# A Morning in Eden

# A Morning in Eden

## Anna Gilbert

St. Martin's Minotaur
New York

www.minotaurbooks.com

ISBN 0-312-28438-1

First published in Great Britain by Robert Hale Limited

First St. Martin's Minotaur Edition: December 2001

10  9  8  7  6  5  4  3  2  1

'There's something strange about this part of the world. Sometimes it's so beautiful' – she stopped, defeated. They could never be described, those breathless moments when the harmony of the earth and sky seemed to have reached such perfection that any change must be discordant. 'It makes me apprehensive.'

'Fair as a morning in Eden,' he said, 'and as old as sin.'

# Chapter 1

They had come too far. For the older ladies, especially for Aunt Belle, this particular Sunday evening walk had been a mistake. Aunt Mabel of course refused to give in: the expedition had been her idea, and her determination alone had got them as far as this, almost to the end of Fold Lane.

Lorna, walking ahead, had already reached the turning where an overgrown track on their left led to their destination, the old Hammond house. Pausing to cast a backward glance and a word of encouragement, she saw Aunt Belle's fair face flushed to purple and ran back, groping in her pocket for the smelling salts.

'You're sadly out of shape for walking.' Mabel watched as her sister took a second grateful sniff. 'You'd better sit on the wall here for a minute and then we'll turn back.'

'I'm sorry, dear. You're disappointed.'

'That's neither here nor there. All I wanted was to see if there'll be a good crop on that apple tree. There isn't a tree in Canterlow that bears as well as that one of the Hammonds – and nobody there to benefit. It does seem a shame.'

'A terrible shame,' Belle echoed, thinking of the three Hammond boys, all killed in the war.

'It's such a good early apple, the Grenadier.'

'But not as tasty as your own Bramley.' Lorna knelt to push

Belle's hat back and gently wipe her forehead with a handkerchief.

'But they're for storing. The Grenadiers are ripe no later than the first week in September as a rule. Never mind. Another day perhaps. Only' – it occurred to her that tomorrow she would be on her own again – 'there's nothing to stop you from going on to the Hammonds' place. It wouldn't take long, you go at such a pace.'

'I'd like to.' Lorna sprang to her feet with the alacrity of a prisoner unexpectedly released.

'You needn't come back this way. You can take one of the field paths and cut across the churchyard – as if you'd gone to look at your Uncle Arthur's grave. You could even be home ahead of us and see that Gladys has the table set and the kettle on the boil.'

But Lorna walked slowly, savouring the bliss of solitude. The annual holiday at Canterlow was almost over. Never once until now had she been free to do as she liked. There were so many other things to be done when staying at The Birches. Ungrudgingly she would so have described the experience of being constantly at Aunt Mabel's beck and call, and was rewarded for her forbearance by the speed with which she forgot her: forgot everything but the stillness of summer trees, the patterns of light and shade on the turf, the scent of wayside flowers. In the absence of other people the natural scene asserted its living presence and transformed her, she felt, into the person she was meant to be.

The green lane became a woodland path and presently the grey walls and stone roof-tiles of the Hammond house appeared between branches. She had been there before but not for a long time; yet there were fewer changes than might have been expected in a house left unoccupied for years and in the middle of a wood, so that instinctively she glanced at the windows as if someone might see her as she picked her way through the overgrown garden, disturbing butterflies, her skirt brushed by rampant valerian, her feet occasionally caught in long stems of periwinkle.

There was no mistaking the tree. Against the warm south-facing wall it promised a crop of Grenadiers to satisfy Aunt Mabel's most extravagant expectations. She plucked one from a low bough. It resisted her twist, a sign of unripeness confirmed when she set her teeth in it and winced.

'Let us hope,' she thought, with what she felt to be sardonic wit, 'that Eve was luckier.' Not that she deserved to be. Never having known temptation – or serpents either for that matter – Lorna had little sympathy for our First Parent, the Mother of us all, whose fatal weakness had caused so much trouble.

But now she was tempted. Having come all this way it seemed a shame not to take a peek inside. The windows had fortified themselves over the years with tangled vines and nettles. Impossible to get near them. In any case the small leaded panes were practically opaque with dirt: it must be almost dark inside. She was a little taken aback to find the front door of heavy oak unlocked. It yielded to a firm push, letting a shaft of light into the dimness of the stone-flagged hall.

'Is there anybody there?'

Only her absolute certainty that there was not gave her courage to call out like that. Had there been a reply she would have taken to her heels or simply died of fright. Even so, she left the door open behind her in preparation for instant flight and stood well away from the walls, with a wary eye on the staircase.

A fireplace occupied most of one wall, its hearth black and empty under a heavy stone mantelpiece. There was no furniture, only a high stool by the window and at the bottom of the stairs a broken Windsor chair; and over all a quietness deep enough to chill the blood of a person standing there alone.

In other circumstances she might have lingered, picturing the place as it ought to be; furnishing the empty hall to her own taste, as if, having lived all her life in someone else's house, she had at last found one of her own. But now there stole upon her a sense of solitude quite different from that of the green lane and its sheltering trees: an awareness of the immense burden of human suffering: of a family bereft of its three sons in the space of two years: of the pitiless waste of life.

Such thoughts left her with no impulse to explore the other rooms as she had half looked forward to doing. The door dragged on the stone flags as she pulled it to, taking a last look round before closing it. In the narrowing shaft of light she caught sight of something on the floor under the window: a small brightness; a man's cuff-link; a square stone of dark red rimmed with gold. She picked it up and put it carefully, as if it mattered, on the window ledge. Because there was nothing else of interest, nothing on which to fix the mind, it became significant like a message. Whereas a moment before she had felt only the void left by the three young men who had gone, leaving no visible trace, here was tangible evidence of a masculine presence. A relic? Or perhaps it had been dropped by an intruder. Whoever was responsible for the house should keep it locked.

Her way home, as she stood with her back to the house, was to the left. Ahead, framed by trees and wonderfully bright after the gloom indoors, an aerial pool of light filled the sky. A few steps forward and she looked down steeply sloping fields to the gleaming water of a dam, now golden as the sky above. On its farther side woodland rose as steeply, its heavy foliage dark against the radiance of sunlight.

It was then that she saw them, halfway down the slope. They stood on one of the paths that intersected the hillside: a girl and a man close together, facing each other. From above she could not see the man clearly – an outspread bough from the ragged hedge of hawthorns partly screened his figure in its Sunday black – nor could she see his face under the brim of a black hat.

It was the girl that she saw and remembered: a girl in a white dress, and rather younger than herself, judging by long hair falling free almost to her waist. Whether actually fair or light brown, the long beams of the westering sun turned it to gold. In white and gold, suffused with light, she looked from this distance – how could one describe her? – ethereal.

They were lovers: there was no doubt of it. Even though they simply stood there – Lorna had seen no embrace – in their closeness and in the girl's attitude of total commitment to her companion without reservation, she sensed an intimacy that set her own heart beating faster. To her, as yet, love was an idea, an ideal; a marvel: a mystery: endlessly fascinating; to be looked forward to, hoped for, discovered some day in a miraculous fulfilment of destiny. She was witnessing the thing itself and ought not to watch.

Then to her dismay – it was distressing to see – the girl raised her arms to her lover's shoulders as if to embrace him. He drew back. She did not let him go but leaned against him as if for the support he seemed to be denying her. Her arms, white and clinging, slid down his rigid black form as the girl herself sank down until she crouched at his feet, head bowed. He stooped. Lorna saw only an arm, a hand, the crown of his black hat as he wrenched apart the hands that fettered him. A moment later he was gone, a moving darkness between green hawthorns.

Alone, on her knees, the girl watched him go. There drifted through the air a thin cry of distress as she sank face-down on the grass, weeping no doubt. But there was no sound of weeping as she got slowly to her feet, no sound at all – no movement except the moving away of a cloud, to leave an extra dazzling brightness on the water. Had the girl seen it as she wiped away tears with the back of her hand? She was looking down at the dam.

It was startling to see her come suddenly and violently to life – to see her running headlong downhill with a reckless disregard of the risk of falling. Lorna was to remember that in spite of her unhappiness she ran with the fluid unconscious ease of youth as if to escape for ever from the scene of her rejection. A low wall marked the end of the pasture. She went over it with scarcely a pause and into the meadow where grass was greening again after the early hay harvest.

From the trees on the opposite hillside came the raucous cry of a jay. A heron rose from the dam and flapped slowly away. It might have been a dream. In dreams one feels more intensely than in waking hours and for a few minutes pity for the girl had been as vivid as the heightened sensation from which one wakes with relief. Now in its frame of arching branches, the picture of golden sky, green earth and bright water was as it had been: undisturbed, unchanged, except for a faintly discernible circle of white on the grass. The girl's hat.

The incident had been no dream. What could be more real than the discovery that love is inseparable from pain? If it's like that, Lorna thought. . . . Is it always like that? Must it be like that?

# Chapter 2

Lorna and her Aunt Belle left for Donnerton early the next morning. 'It's been very nice.' Belle settled snugly in her seat as the train steamed out. 'But a fortnight is long enough.'

'You say that every year. I wonder if Aunt Mabel feels the same about her fortnight with us at Christmas.'

'Perhaps. There's no place like home. Oh, I know that's a hackneyed thing to say but it's true.'

No. 3 Princes Crescent was certainly her home: she had been born there; and she would have been hurt by any suggestion that it was not also the home of her niece, who had been with her from infancy. Lorna's mother had died in childbirth. The aunts had rallied to the crisis with such dutiful willingness that by the time she was five, her father had felt free to escape to West Virginia and a share in a small coal mine. Lorna was to remain with her aunts until she was old enough to keep house for him. But before she had attained that useful age he had married again and gave no sign of returning, though the £50 he allowed annually for her maintenance was paid into the bank at Donnerton with unfailing regularity.

Lorna had never known Aunt Mabel's husband who died when she was two, but she was forever grateful to him for having lived long enough to prevent Aunt Mabel from taking her in. Or on? Arthur could scarcely be expected, his wife argued reasonably, to shoulder the burden of a newborn child not his own, when Belle, still a spinster, had the old family house in Donnerton with eight rooms all to herself and would be all the better for her niece's company in the years to come.

And so she was. Belle had been blessed with a serenity of temperament and lightness of heart denied to her sister Mabel, who was inclined to disapprove of her manner as being too girl-ish for a middle-aged woman. Perhaps only Lorna knew that the apparent lightness was counterbalanced by more serious moods though even she never penetrated their depths.

Aunt and niece were happy together, their relationship a rare blend of motherly care, daughterly trust and sisterly comrade-ship, and they were able to feel sorry for Mabel, widowed in her early thirties and childless – or to put it more precisely – to feel that Mabel had not been improved by the misfortune of having to live alone.

Nevertheless, though No. 3 Princes Crescent had all the advantages of a home and was so indistinguishable from a real one that Lorna never consciously thought about it, there lurked at the back of her mind an awareness that the security it offered was conditional: she was there because of Aunt Belle's goodness of heart which she must in some way acknowledge. How? By being useful? The charmless word was often on Aunt Mabel's lips and Lorna, who thought of herself as being unremarkable in every way, cheerfully accepted it as a way of describing herself. It was no trouble to be useful. For the time being there was noth-ing else she passionately wanted to be.

'There's more in life than being useful,' Aunt Belle decreed when the topic was once broached. 'We must each live in accord-ance with our own nature.'

Such remarks, inspired by novels borrowed from Heath's Lending Library, occasionally enriched their conversation. 'Little did we think' or 'Alas, it was not to be' applied to a dis-appointment over a picnic or a failed omelette gave a kind of bogus stateliness to a humdrum situation. Aunt Belle was probably the only person in Donnerton who used the words 'Alas', 'deemed' and 'nonetheless'.

'There are times,' she told Lorna 'when one must rise a little above the merely commonplace,' and she would gaze for a moment or two into the middle distance as if recalling a way of life not to be found in Donnerton, though she had in fact never lived anywhere else and had never strayed much farther than Canterlow. Lorna paid heed (as Belle would have put it) and sympathized but was not deceived, recognizing such a mood as the flutter of wings of a caged bird. From Aunt Belle she learned that one can live on more than one level.

Lorna was interested in other people, less disposed to talk about herself. But in her quiet attentiveness there was an awareness that, as Aunt Belle declared, 'Things are not always what they seem to be – or people'. It was a question of using one's common sense, Lorna supposed, being as yet ignorant of its extreme limitations in dealing with human problems.

Her sense of indebtedness was perhaps more deeply ingrained because, as she came to realize, her very life had been granted at the expense of her mother's. It was chastening to think that if she had not existed, her mother would have continued to do so. An actor whose appearance on the stage coincides with the exit of a more important player need not expect to be greeted with a round of applause and may not necessarily be taken to the hearts of the audience. Moreover her grasp of the plot and meaning of the drama may be less confident than that of players who have managed things less awkwardly.

At the very beginning she had undoubtedly suffered a loss. The first natural bond had been broken. To emerge from the womb not into the maternal arms but into the arms of an aunt – indeed the arms of two aunts – may induce an unconscious hesitation. Though, on the other hand it is said that what you never have you never miss, the proposition is hard to prove. Mercifully, in Lorna's early years the floodtide of psychology had not yet engulfed the general public. There were still enlightened people who had never heard of Freud or of inhibitions or neuroses; nor was it in Lorna's nature to brood over so distant an event as her birth.

'Be thankful you're alive,' Aunt Belle said, Lorna's reference to it having sounded faintly apologetic. 'You might have gone too and what would I have done all alone without you?' It was spoken from the heart and not in the manner of Miss Braddon or Marie Corelli.

To have saved Aunt Belle from a life of solitude had entailed no sacrifice. It was Aunt Mabel who, dipping into the future, hinted at problems as yet unforeseen.

'She may marry, I suppose, though she doesn't seem given that way, and then you'll know what it's like to be on your own,' she told her sister more than once. 'But there'll always be a home for you at The Birches when she does, and most of your furniture can be fitted in somehow except great-grandmother Featherstone's long-case clock. It's far too tall for my ceilings. But those balls could be taken off the top, I dare say, and it should be kept in the family.'

On such occasions as the conversation wandered off into the distribution of Aunt Belle's furniture in the event, unlikely as yet, of her own marriage, Lorna felt depressed and even, when very young, shed a tear or two for Aunt Belle, doomed either to solitude or to giving up her home. Not even to secure one for herself could she abandon her to such a fate.

'Don't worry,' she promised earnestly at the age of ten. 'I'll never get married.' At that stage in her life it seemed the least she could do to give up all hope of a home of her own in order to safeguard Aunt Belle's. Not until much later did it dawn on her that as her aunt – though prettier and altogether more pleasing than most women, than Aunt Mabel for instance – had never married, it was obviously possible to have a home without the bother of a husband.

So far, until her nineteenth year, the problem had been theoretical: no ardent suitor had materialized to urge her into wedlock; none of the young men of their acquaintance would have appealed to her in such a role and that was a pity, as events were to prove.

Miss Featherstone and Miss Kent were popular in Donnerton where even in wartime there were social gatherings of a kind to satisfy their modest demands: concerts with collections for the war effort, weddings, dances for servicemen home on leave and summer day-trips to the seaside. No. 3 could be counted on to accommodate sewing meetings as well as for its tea parties. The house was pleasant and comfortable, the solid furnishings of earlier Featherstones garnished with Belle's softening touches: lace table mats, flower-painted china, shell-covered boxes, embroidered fire screens and paintings of ringleted children with wide-eyed kittens. Its solid foundations included Aggie in the kitchen. Now in her fifties, she had spent the greater part of her life there.

Their particular friends were the Liffeys. Lorna's grandfather and a contemporary Liffey had been partners in a small blade and cutlery firm and the connection continued after his death. In the wartime shortage of staff Belle stepped in as a part-time clerk. The present Mrs Liffey suspected her of being 'flighty' in her book-keeping but there were no complaints and Belle loved being the one to pay out the weekly wages. Lorna helped in a crèche for infants of working mothers.

The tranquil days flowed smoothly. Only in retrospect did Lorna realize how happy they had been. The discomfort Belle had suffered on that Sunday evening walk at Canterlow should have been seen as a warning.

On a winter afternoon in the New Year, 1919, they were in the attic together rummaging for contributions to a sale of bygones, the proceeds to establish a second crèche. Stocks had been depleted in November for jumble sales in aid of the Armistice celebrations, but there were still bygones enough for any number of sales. Relics of Featherstones long-dead bulged from trunks and boxes: dresses, capes, curtains, bed linen, bundles of letters. It should have been fun. For Lorna the long, low space under the roof had been a treasure house to explore on wet days and later the setting for sentimental porings over snippets of family history. But at that dead time of the year both were tired and the attic was cold.

'We're not making much progress.' She yawned, yearning for tea and toast by the dining-room fire.

'We must be firm, no turning back. That's how we won the war, remember. It's absurd to keep all this stuff. Let's make a clean sweep.'

But neither of them was in the mood, even if a clean sweep of decades of clutter had been possible.

'I suppose this could go.' Lorna held it up rather regretfully: a mauve dolman with gilt buttons. 'And this': a petticoat of yellowing white with nine inches of embroidery round the hem.

'And what about this?' Belle put it on: an Edwardian hat, wide-brimmed, heavily swathed in tulle, in its folds sprays of rosebuds and lily-of-the-valley. She bent the brim to frame her face and assumed a suitable expression, soulful and remote. 'A garden party perhaps.'

'Or a wedding. I wonder whose. . . .' Lorna broke off. Belle's face had changed. She had let go of the hat and clutched her side. Released, the brim resumed its wide span leaving her face fully exposed. 'You're tired. We shouldn't have moved those heavy trunks.' She had never seen Belle looking like that. Perhaps she had caught the influenza. There was so much of it about. 'It's too cold for you up here. Go down, do. I'll put a few things together. Oh, what is it? You're ill.'

She dropped the petticoat, stumbling in its folds as she rushed to her aunt – to help her, to hold her up. Her whole body seemed contorted with pain, one shoulder high as she gripped her upper arm. But when Lorna tried to ease her so that she could at least lean against one of the trunks, Belle shook her head as if she couldn't bear to be touched.

'I'll get brandy.'

'No time.' The voice was almost soundless. 'Lorna. I'm going. . . .'

'You can't. Dearest, you can't. . . .'

The ridiculous hat had slipped askew, its frivolous concoction of tulle and flowers obscene in those moments of stark reality. She took it off and threw it away, leaned closer and with a sudden terrible foreknowledge of loneliness to come, looked into her aunt's eyes and saw in their fading blue a loneliness more dire: the ultimate loneliness of the dying.

'You'll be . . . Mabel. . . .' The gasp grew fainter. Then with a last glint of life before the final agony seized her – 'A good heart . . . better than this one of mine.'

A minute later Lorna saw her die. Still holding her, she sat on under the darkening skylight, indifferent to the cold, numbed as she was by the far more bitter chill of a changed world in which there was no one left for her to love.

After a while she laid Belle down among the discarded dresses and the scattered photographs of forgotten people, went down to the landing and called Aggie.

# Chapter 3

Aunt Mabel went home after the funeral, having advised Lorna on every detail of the packing up and disposal of goods and chattels.

'She needn't have bothered,' Aggie said. After thirty-one years in the same house she had become much more than a servant. 'We'll just do what Miss Belle would have wanted.'

But like Lorna she was too dispirited to initiate a mutiny. Together they dismantled the eight rooms and sent the last of the furniture to a saleroom. Everything of value had been dispatched to Canterlow: the clock with its balls and finials in a separate box and its weights in another; the mahogany tallboy; the suite from the best bedroom; the cradle in which the three Featherstone sisters and Lorna herself had been rocked – ('You may have children of your own some day,' Aunt Mabel said, though still comfortably convinced that Lorna was not the marrying kind) – and all the china and household linen; crochet-edged tablecloths and tray-cloths, bed valances and embroidered guest towels from the hands of great-aunts and two grandmothers; four wicker baskets of objects to be kept in the family; the family Bible; a *Pilgrim's Progress* and a leather-bound set of the twenty-five Waverley novels.

Friends were kind. On the last day a stream of visitors dropped in to say goodbye.

'Living in the country will be as good as a holiday,' Rita Liffey said, having exhausted all other means of consolation. 'Clean and healthy and quiet. There'll be none of the soot and muck we have to put up with here. There's as much dust to wipe off the window-sills every day as you would find in a coal cellar.'

'I do like the country,' Lorna said, her tone dismal.

'You may not have the soot and dirt,' Faith Wilbur told her, 'but you'll be lucky if you find the same kindness. Sometimes the people who have the most to put up with are the first to know when help is needed and do their best to give it.'

She spent most of her time in the poorer quarters of the city and knew what she was talking about. Lorna's affection for her was tinged with awe: it was an effort to live up to the standard Faith set for herself. She came of a wealthy Quaker family and could have lived a life of ease such as most young women would have envied.

'But you'll find friends wherever you go, Lorna,' she said, regretting her last remark. 'I was being peevish because I'm going to miss you. I'd been counting on you to take on the next crèche and run it yourself. You'd do it so well.'

She picked up the bulging leather bag she carried everywhere, a quaint little figure well known in Donnerton, her skirts, drab grey or brown, an inch or two shorter than was fashionable. They were precautionary like her thick black boots. In some of the places she visited there was much to avoid treading on.

'We must keep in touch.' She kissed Lorna who had seen her to the front door, and went off briskly to a meeting of likely contributors to a fund for the maintenance of a nursing home for war widows, wondering as she dodged a brewer's dray to board her tram, how much longer she could go on being brisk and sensible and whether as a cure for heartache her relentless busyness was having the slightest effect. There were days when her enthusiasm failed her, when the burden of human misery, including her own, seemed too heavy to bear. To give one's whole life to helping other people to bear theirs would be to do no more than nibble at the huge impenetrable mass of it. Yet to give up the nibbling would be the worst punishment she could inflict on herself, an endless succession of empty days, long years of loneliness.

The recent conversation had unsettled her: it had reminded her of how much she too loved the country. On the Sussex downs with larks rising, in flower-deep meadows, in the garden where she and Henry had said goodbye in the soft twilight – it was there that she felt closest to him, there he was almost within reach. But the stronger the sense of his nearness, the more agonizing the pain of his loss. Where there was nothing to distract her from thinking of him, there was no relief either from the aching knowledge that she would never see him again. On that ancient landscape, unchanged and unchanging, they had left less trace than a swiftly passing cloud shadow. It was over.

'Now then. Miss Wilbur.' The conductor took her three ha'pence and punched a ticket. 'You'd be better at home today. There'll be a fair bit of slush down at Brandon – and plenty of flu about. You'll need to be careful.'

'I'll be careful.' She made the transition from Sussex in summertime to a January day in Brandon, a poverty-stricken district in the gloom of steelworks – made it without effort and remembered Lorna, whose transition would be in the opposite direction, from town to country. She knew that her own romantic memories bore no relation to the realities of existence in the country. There could be as many problems in rural life as in Donnerton, some of them less obvious and so more difficult to solve. In cities human beings created their own environment, scarred and ugly as it too often was. But in the country the environment shaped the people. Momentarily she saw them as victims, exposed to Nature's fearsome blend of cruelty and beauty, unchangeable and unimpaired.

It was a theory she and Henry had wrangled over and

dismissed as too vague to have any foundation in fact. If there should be anything to worry about, Lorna would find it out for herself. All the same there was perhaps something more she could have said, some advice she could have given. About what? She really didn't know. Yet instinctively – for she was not always reasonable – she had felt the need to protect the girl, who was after all completely alone in the world. Without compunction Faith swept aside Aunt Mabel as a nonentity so far as sympathetic understanding was concerned and of no more use than a remorselessly absent father; and then in response to the twang of the bell at the next stop, she stepped down cautiously into the soot-blackened slush of a narrow pavement. . . .

'I must be going too,' Rita was saying. 'By the way, I've just remembered. Wasn't it at Canterlow that they found that man's body? A man called Ezra or some such name. There was a bit about it in the *Gazette*. He had fallen over a cliff in a snow storm. They didn't find him until the snow melted. Nobody knew how he got there – or when.'

'That's one thing that couldn't have happened in Donnerton,' her brother Cedric reminded her. 'It would be noticed.' One dead man with all that space to himself! He moved to the window and looked out, remembering what had happened to most of his platoon at the St Quentin canal.

The house was unheated. Bare walls and uncarpeted floors gave little encouragement to linger over leave-taking. Only Cedric stayed on when the others had gone. All the chairs had gone too. Having helped to buckle its leather straps, he sat down on a dress basket. Lorna perched on the chilly windowsill with her back to a sky heavy with snow. They waited for the taxi. Cedric would look after her luggage and see her off at the station.

'It's a big step you're taking, leaving Donnerton and all your friends,' he said after a silence in which there had been no awkwardness: they had known each other all their lives.

'There wasn't much choice.'

'You'll be feeling the way I did when I was demobbed, coming home hasn't been what I expected. Everything seems to have changed. People too.'

It was not easy to describe the difference between the home-coming he had dreamed of in the stinking trenches and the shock of its reality. After the ceaseless pounding of gunfire Donnerton seemed at first strangely quiet, its citizens absorbed in a variety of pointless pursuits. In France the choice had been narrower: kill or be killed.

'Friends don't change.' Lorna spoke mechanically, still wondering where she had put the key of the china cabinet. It would have arrived at The Birches locked and, without the key, must remain so, forever empty.

'You're right, Lorna.' Cedric had brightened. He was a well-built young man, slow and careful in speech and movement as befitted a craftsman used to handling sharp blades. 'Friends don't change – and I dare say you'll come back now and again.'

'There won't be anything to come back to.' The dress basket with Cedric on it wavered through sudden tears.

Yet from the moment of her arrival at Canterlow she missed Donnerton; missed Aggie almost as much as she missed Aunt Belle; missed Faith and the Liffeys, even Cedric. Her bedroom at The Birches, crammed with objects she had lived with for years, gave her no sense of belonging. If life in Donnerton had ever seemed to an observer drab and lacking in glamour, Lorna had not found it so. A party, a concert, an occasional dance had provided the nearest approach to a thrill she had ever experienced. Talking things over with Aunt Belle after each event had given an added relish which they both enjoyed. Their life had been safe and easy with a sparkle of fun.

Its end had come like a thunderbolt followed by a falling apart; a collapse of walls and ceilings: the erosion of familiar pavements; and somewhere, uneasily reft from the living world, her blue eyes strained as in her last attack, Aunt Belle looked down in dismay, interested but unreachable.

Now there was only Aunt Mabel. Lorna edged between bags, trunks and an excess of furniture and began to unpack. The key of the china cabinet was in her dressing-gown pocket. Things might have been worse.

# Chapter 4

Among the ladies of Canterlow it was generally agreed that Mrs Hobcroft had improved since her niece came to live with her. She had previously been rather too much on her high horse.

'The loss of her sister has had a softening effect,' was the more charitable verdict of the minister's wife. 'She is mellowing as we all hope to do in growing older.'

If Mabel Hobcroft had not come down from her high horse for good, she had evidently seen the necessity of alighting from time to time. Her sister's death had indeed been a sad blow from which she was slow to recover. Meanwhile there had been time to realize the many advantages of having Lorna with her and the desirability of keeping her there. Though it had not yet occurred to Lorna, it had not been lost on her aunt that with the £500 Belle had left her in her will and the yearly allowance from her father, recently increased, she was not dependent on her aunt or on The Birches for her home. Moreover it would be just like Bernard Kent to offer her a home in West Virginia whenever it suited him, without consideration for others who had taken on the responsibility he had shuffled off.

She was beginning to realize that Lorna was not the girl she had been – or had seemed to be – on those fortnightly holidays when she had been very much the third and junior member of the trio. She had become less . . . more. . . . It was difficult to say what she had become except that she was no longer – if she ever had been – insignificant.

How indeed could one describe the effect on Lorna of the speed with which she had been thrust into maturity, of Belle's abrupt departure, of the sudden onset of loneliness? She had come face to face with death and had learned from it that living must entail more than submission to a motiveless sequence of days. There must be something more. Seeking a new direction, she moved in uncharted spiritual waters and there were times when she simply ceased to notice Aunt Mabel, forgot even that she was there.

But Mabel was very definitely there. She too felt the need of a new direction for her niece though of a less intangible kind. Lorna must be encouraged to settle in Canterlow. She must be drawn into things, acclimatized, pinned down. The pinning down began one morning at breakfast.

'I was thinking that you might take on the collecting for the War Widows and Orphans Fund, for this month at any rate. I've been doing it since it was started. It's such a good cause.'

It would get her out of the house and give her an interest. That she herself would be relieved of a tiresome duty was neither here nor there. In fact she was genuinely anxious to see an improvement in Lorna's health and spirits. They had now been together for two months. Country air, fresh milk and cream and Mabel's well-supplied table had done little to bring colour to her cheeks or even to fill them out a little.

Her eyes were now pensive: beautiful eyes of a luminous grey. She took after the Kents in looks. Her father – though Mabel had not much use for him – was a handsome man. Lorna had inherited his slimness, symmetry of features and dark hair and when she smiled, her face lit up with a sort of inner radiance. The phrase was fanciful. It had been one of Belle's.

'You would get to know people.'

'Yes.' Lorna was not unwilling, nor was she enthusiastic. It was

28

the sort of thing she had been doing for years and was evidently doomed to go on doing for ever. Obviously Aunt Mabel was sick of it and who could blame her. 'Tell me what to do,' she continued.

'It's for money and comforts. I'll give you a list. You could do the other side this morning.'

'The other side' was the older part of Canterlow beyond the little river Beam which divided the town socially as well as geographically. Lorna paused on the bridge to consult her list. The stream below was full and fast flowing, swollen by melted snow on the high moorland it had left. Snowdrops grew thick on its bank; buds would soon be thickening on the alders. Looking down over the parapet, she saw a kingfisher dart to cover. It was mid-morning; the streets were quiet, the children in school.

Raven Terrace, Aunt Mabel had said, was usually worth visiting. They were nice people there except for one house on its own behind a wall. 'Don't bother with the Hoods. They're best left alone.'

She began at the top of the street and worked her way down, by which time both tin and basket were heavy enough to justify going home. There had been no need to introduce herself: she was recognized and welcomed as a pleasant change from her aunt. At more than one house she was invited in and offered a cup of tea with snatches of local news. It was in quite a cheerful mood that she approached the last house, set down the heavy basket on the step and knocked.

'They won't come to the door.'

It was a girl's voice, close at hand. Lorna had not noticed her: small wonder as she sat close to the garden wall, hunched up and clasping her knees. Her loose grey dress was almost the same colour as the stones, so that she seemed to emanate from the wall or to have grown on it like colourless lichen, Lorna thought, half amused, half repelled.

'You can knock as hard as you like but they won't answer.'

Only then did it occur to her that 'they' must be the Hoods whom she had been warned not to bother with.

'Then I won't disturb them,' she said. 'There must be illness in the house or perhaps they're very old.'

'There's nobody ill and nobody old.'

Lorna was intrigued. The stark statements and the cool emotionless voice were as impersonal as those of an oracle. And the girl herself? She appeared to be about fourteen years old, thin to the point of peakiness, with a pointed chin that made her face seem long, and hair dragged back by a black band. The most distinctive thing about her was the unusual whiteness of her skin. Her eyebrows were fair and just distinguishable in their leprous setting which made her eyes of mid-blue seem richer and deeper in colour than they actually were and her thin lips, of a normal redness, seem blood-red. The effect, in the absence of any other expression to counteract it, was of a latent ferocity unusual in a girl or in anyone at all for that matter.

Lorna felt no qualms in looking at her more curiously than was polite: the girl was as indifferent and self-contained as a sphinx, or as a gargoyle on the wall behind her. Her hands were white like her face but with a bluish tinge.

'Aren't you cold, sitting there?'

'Yes.'

'Why not go home and get warm?'

'I am at home.'

'Have you been locked out?' For some misdemeanour perhaps. She looked capable of almost anything, so complete was her disregard of normal behaviour.

'I can get in when I want but I like being outside.'

It didn't sound right. To get in was not quite the same as to go in. One tried to get into a fortress or a shop after closing hours. One simply went home.

'I think you should move about and get your circulation going. Run up and down – or something,' Lorna ended lamely, aware of the unsuitability of such activity in one who had never been young. That was it. She was too self-sufficient, too strangely knowing ever to have been young.

She picked up her basket and was surprised when the girl uncurled herself, with some difficulty – how long had she been sitting there, for goodness' sake? – and joined her on the path.

'They never let me go anywhere,' she said, 'so I sneak out when I can.'

Lorna looked back at the windows. She had stood at a projecting porch and had not noticed that all the blinds were down. There must have been a bereavement.

'I'm Lorna Kent,' she said. 'What's your name?'

'Etta Hood.'

'Why don't you walk a little way with me?' she said and instantly regretted the suggestion. They must have some reason for keeping the girl indoors. Was she crazy? A glance at the girl's face, level with her own shoulder, provided no answer. The face was closed, expressionless – which didn't mean that its owner might not suddenly explode into some irrational act. She resolved to keep their walk short and find an excuse for sending, or if necessary taking her home. And suddenly, sure enough, the girl sprang in front of her on the pavement and walking backwards, stared up at her.

'You're pretty,' she said. 'So you'd better be careful.' In some weird fashion her voice changed in pitch and tone. 'A good looking girl needs to keep herself *to* herself.'

It was a quotation, a mimicry, a clue of sorts.

'Does anybody else live in your house beside you and them?'

She had made a false move. The girl stopped so abruptly that she had to stop too.

'No. Nobody else.' She spat out the words with violence and yet there was desolation too in her voice. 'There's nobody else now but me and them.'

Without another word she ran back to the house and disappeared. Presumably her way of getting in was at the back. She had vanished like a lost soul into an element one could only guess at. That was an exaggeration of course but Lorna was left with a disturbing impression of unhappiness, accepted by the sufferer as a condition one could do nothing about. She was too young to feel like that, certainly too young to be kept away from other girls. Ought she not to be at school? The silent house with all the blinds drawn was cheerless even to an outsider.

It would have been interesting to hear more about the Hoods, but by the time she reached home her aunt had already left after an early lunch to attend a meeting of the school managers, from which she returned with news of more immediate interest to them both.

The headmaster, Mr Ushart, was in difficulties. One of the women teachers was ill and would be away for some time. Her work would be shared among other members of staff but there would be no one to supervise the girls' needlework.

'Two afternoons a week. Only for a while of course. I did say that you might be interested.'

'But I have no qualifications, either for teaching or needlework.'

'You're clever with your needle. That jacket you made me could have come from the hands of a professional dressmaker. I know of no one who can set a sleeve better, and if you can set a sleeve and fit a collar you can do anything.'

Even more important, according to Mr Ushart, was that the person who would spend two afternoons a week with the girls should be suitable in character and background.

' "And if there is any person in Canterlow or elsewhere with a background superior to that of my niece or a better character", I told him, "I should like to know who that person is." . . . I've been a school manager longer than anyone but the vicar and I do feel an obligation to come to the rescue in a crisis like this. And,' she added, 'twenty-five shillings a calendar month is not to be sneezed at.'

'Well, if there really is no one else. . . .'

Lorna had not met the headmaster but she knew enough about him to feel some trepidation as she walked down Abbot's Lane that afternoon. He was so very highly thought of. In Aunt Mabel's opinion, Mr Ushart did more for the town than the vicar, even more than the minister, though as a Wesleyan she was loath to say so. It would be a sad loss if ever he moved to a bigger school.

The lane dipped downhill, then climbed to the Abbey Farm. At its lowest point Lorna had her first glimpse of the school on her right against a background of trees. She had not been prepared for the rustic charm of its situation. Snug in its leafy hollow, it seemed, with schoolhouse, garden and orchard, to have withdrawn into a region of its own, timeless and exclusive – a harmonious blend of grey walls and roof-tiles and boughs still bare against a sky of tender blue.

The church clock struck four and in swift response there floated through open windows the sound of singing:

'Lord, keep us safe this night,
Secure from all our fears. . . .'

The voices, thin and not quite in unison, were unaccompanied; but presently an unseen pianist struck up a brisk marching tune and the two main doors opened, disgorging the juvenile population of Canterlow. Lorna waited outside the gate until the hubbub died down and the lane was empty, and she was still hesitating when two women carrying attaché cases came out.

'Mr Ushart? You'll find him in the hall.'

They were followed by a young man, black-haired, sallow-skinned, with a pile of exercise books held loosely under his arm. One or two of them slipped as he attempted to put on his hat. Clutching at them, he dislodged the whole pile.

'Oh, I say, it's awfully good of you.'

His worried frown was rather touching. Lorna had picked up

some of the books and now dusted them with her handkerchief and arranged them in an orderly pile as he retrieved the others. He murmured something about the handle of a case having come off, attempted once more to deal with his hat but desisted, to her relief, and shuffled off, his frayed trouser hems trailing over his boots.

Beyond a cloakroom with pegs and benches an inner door stood open. She could see into the hall. Mr Ushart sat at his desk, neither writing nor reading. In profile the droop of his mouth was stern – or sad. His hands were tightly folded above papers. He was staring down at them as if lost in thought.

He had not heard her quiet approach. She knocked. He got up quickly.

'Mr Ushart.'

He saw a slim young woman in mourning. Her face was pale, clear in outline, he thought with the detachment of a stranger, and lit by rather fine grey eyes. They were more deeply under-lined, their lids heavier than they should have been, from sleep-lessness perhaps or weeping: he knew that she had been through a difficult time. But he recognized in them a youthful openness to experience and their gaze was steadfast in spite of her obvious nervousness. Whatever had happened to her so far had not been more than she could deal with; she was grief-stricken perhaps but not distressed.

'My aunt, Mrs Hobcroft, told me. . . .'

'Of course. You are Miss Kent.'

He placed a chair for her and remained standing. He was above medium height and sparely built. At that first meeting she thought of him as middle-aged. He was thirty-eight.

'And you think you may be able to help us?'

She had intended to ask sensible questions, still uncertain as to whether to commit herself. Instead she listened, her eyes on his face as he told her what would be required. Her role would be little more than to supervise and help. She liked his voice –

34

which was low-pitched and pleasant to listen to – and the way he put things. After all he was an educated man. It was uncomfortable to feel that he must be summing her up. Was she suitable? For a moment the simple task of helping girls with their needlework swelled to the proportions of an affair of state. Well, it didn't really matter if he did think her unsuitable. Sitting upright and rigid, she imagined herself rising and bidding him good afternoon with just a hint of coolness before walking, rejected but unhurried, to the door.

His hair was dark and that made his eyes unexpected. They were not large but so unusually light in colour – a greenish hazel – that they shone disconcertingly from under black brows. One had to notice them. She had not expected him to look so like an artist. Or a poet? Her acquaintance with artists was limited to one lecture delivered by a local watercolourist at the City Art Gallery. As for poets, she had seen a picture of Shelley. Based on such meagre evidence, her judgement was no more than instinctive, though the face was indeed mobile and expressive. His manner was rather curt and she felt that he was disinclined to spend more time on her than was necessary. What had seemed a crisis to Aunt Mabel might to a man seem of only moderate importance.

'You'll come?'

'Yes.'

'Tomorrow?' She nodded. 'Good.' He came with her to the outer door. Beyond the playground a gate opened on the garden and orchard. Between them a path led up to the schoolhouse, and she felt again a sense of completion, as in a picture where every feature is drawn into harmony by the artist's hand and eye. She turned impulsively.

'It's perfect, as if it has all been here from the beginning and has never changed. A separate little world in itself. Perhaps it never will change although everything else seems to.'

The moment of insight illuminated her face. He saw the light fade as she became conscious of her loss of restraint – and he was sorry.

'I'm glad you like it.' He smiled and she felt at ease. 'But the beginning was only one hundred and fifty years ago.' He walked with her to the lane. The school, he told her, had been built within reach of the cottages, which in those days together with a few farms constituted the whole of Canterlow. With the coming of steam power the small family forges on the banks of the Beam had been replaced by bigger concerns. The population had increased, the centre of village life had moved eastward towards the high road, more houses had been built. . . .

'Like The Birches.'

'Ah – The Birches. Does the name strike you as rather punitive?'

'I believe it always has.' The discovery amused her. 'Actually the birches were felled ages ago but Aunt Mabel likes the name and wouldn't dream of changing it.'

'And you approve? You dislike change.'

'Not always. Only when things are so beautiful that change might spoil them.'

A chaffinch swooped to within inches of her feet as she went up the lane; aconites glowed under the trees. Was there already a feeling of spring in the air? For the first time since coming to Canterlow she felt a strong upward surge of spirit: a feeling of being herself again.

After she left he stood for a while before going back to his desk. He had sensed in the girl an essential quietness of spirit. For her the tumult and the heat, the grim ordeal of getting from the cradle to the grave, were still to come. She has it all still to face, he thought with a touch of regret and the inward equivalent of a shrug.

'It's perfect,' she had said, her eyes alight. How could she be expected to know the flaws and complexities of the separate little world into which she had found her way? 'Perhaps it never will change although everything else seems to.' Some things are better left unsaid. It was unwise, he could have told her, to challenge the unseen forces that govern human affairs: they can be swift to respond.

But she had reminded him that Canterlow, compared with every other place on earth, was least likely to change. Situated in one of the deep valleys in the southern Pennines, it had taken centuries to evolve from the first primitive settlement into a small twentieth-century market town of no account whatsoever. And the people? Put them back in caves and some of them would quickly revert to the habits and attitudes of their ancestors. Nothing short of an earthquake or a thunderbolt hurled directly from the hand of the Almighty would really change the place. What in heaven's name was he doing there?

For a moment he dwelt with relish on the possibility – in the hope even since there was no other hope – that some violent concussion of nature would rescue him. But it was only for a moment. He returned to his desk, carefully read, sorted and dockcted the various papers there, placed them in the appropriate drawers and with a soft cloth kept for the purpose, swept the desk-top clean, leaving it bare and shining. If he had smiled during these operations, it would not have been from pleasure though he was by nature meticulously tidy; nor would it have been the kind of smile that had set Lorna at her ease. It would have been more like the grimace of a prisoner defying captivity but without hope of release.

# Chapter 5

Lorna was to look back with affection on her afternoons in the classroom. For most of the girls, needlework lessons were an escape from the drudgery of arithmetic, maps, dates of kings and battles, and writing compositions. Slates wiped clean and put away, hands washed, hair tied back, they assembled in the end classroom, consciously superior to the boys who were hammering and sawing in their woodwork lesson or getting their hands and boots dirty in the garden. Whispering was allowed as they sewed but the fourteen-year-olds were anxious to finish their nightdresses or petticoats before leaving at Easter and were less inclined to chatter than in lessons where talking was forbidden.

They had been well taught. The youngest girls knew the basic stitches, could hem and seam and sew on buttons: the older ones could cut out, use the treadle machine and do simple embroidery. It was at the end of her first week, as she and Miss Prior were putting on their coats to go home, that Lorna had asked about Miss Webber.

'Do you know when she will be coming back?'

'*If* she comes back.' Miss Prior was a plain, drably dressed woman in her forties who had taken the newcomer under her wing.

'You think she may not? Then it's serious.'

'Consumption. It's in the family. They're sending her to a sanatorium at Gorsham. She's been threatened with it for years but it does seem to take hold at the age she is now.'

'I should have liked to know her.'

'I'm going to call at the Webbers now. Why not come with me?'

The house was in Victoria Terrace. Mrs Webber made them welcome, showed them into the sitting room and excused herself; she was busy in the kitchen.

The young woman on the sofa though thin and frail had the vivacity that often accompanies the disease and was touchingly pleased to see them.

'Now, Nora, you'll guess who this is.'

'No need to guess. It's Miss Kent for sure.'

'I've been wanting to meet you. You know I'm no expert, not a teacher at all, but I hope not to let you down.'

'Oh, I hear a few things. Sally Buckler brought her nightdress to show me. Not a stitch out of place so far.'

They stayed for ten minutes to chat. Miss Prior passed on all the news, chiefly about the exasperating Mr Moxby, his tiresomeness over sharing the globe, his utter carelessness about pen nibs, for which she was responsible. . . .

'And the look of him, no better than a tramp. He isn't fit to be in charge of children.'

'I never knew a person go downhill as fast as he's done in this last year. He wasn't such a bad sort when he first came, you must admit – with such good testimonials from the College as well.'

'All I know is that nobody but Mr Ushart would put up with him, but you know what he's like. He'll never harden his heart and get rid of Roy Moxby even if he goes clean off the rails.'

'And what about you know who?'

'Nothing's changed so far as I know and never will.'

'Isn't it a shame?'

Lorna listened with interest but remained unenlightened and Miss Prior moved on to another topic.

'This *will* surprise you, Nora. Guess who's turned up again this very day. You could have knocked me down with a feather. I caught sight of her in the end room. No, Miss Kent, I wasn't spying – just happened to be passing. And there she was in the back row with her sewing bag as if she'd never been away.'

'Not Etta Hood? Yes? Well! I wonder why she's condescended to come back.'

'No one ever knew what went on in that girl's head. It's no wonder though, is it, when you think. . . .'

'Perhaps not.'

'Oh, Miss Prior.' In her confusion Lorna had heard little more than the girl's name. 'What must you think of me? I simply didn't see her. I spent so much time showing Emily Farrar how to do French knots – never thought of counting the girls.'

The other two were amused.

'Don't let that worry you. Etta Hood had put herself in the back row where she wouldn't be noticed. . . .'

'And they all look alike in their pinafores, especially as you hardly know them yet.'

'But I do know Etta Hood. At least I saw her. She puzzled me rather. Is there something strange about the family?'

'They've had problems.' Miss Prior gave her a meaningful look and got up. 'We've stayed long enough. Nora's had enough talk for the time being.'

Nora protested but she was firm. Outside in the street she was less restrained.

'In her condition she's easily depressed and the Hoods are a depressing subject. You asked if there was something strange about them.'

It was a sad story. They were an old family: there had always been Hoods in Canterlow. The parents were devout, chapel-going folk and had brought up their two daughters in the utmost respectability. Nevertheless Alice, the elder girl, had got into trouble. Nobody could fathom how such a thing could happen in such a family or who the man could be. The shame had been too much for her father who was much older than his wife. He had not stirred from the house since the affair had become the talk of Canterlow.

The family had shrunk into its shell. Etta was not allowed out on her own and had herself refused to come to school. In the circumstances the Attendance Officer had turned a blind eye. Mrs Hood was trying to arrange a removal to London where she had relatives. It was not easy but they would be leaving Canterlow as soon as possible.

'Everyone was sorry for them although some said there was such a thing as being too strict. But Alice was such a good girl, one of my favourites when she was at school, I must admit. Nothing flighty about her. Quiet, nicely spoken. And lovely long fair hair always smooth and shining like silk. . . .'

'But surely. . . .' Lorna was a little surprised that the affair had raised quite such a stir. It certainly was dreadful especially for such very respectable people. But it had happened in other families. They made the best of it and lived down the disgrace. She had known a girl in Donnington. 'It was a soldier. He was killed before they could be married. . . .'

She was halted by something in Miss Prior's manner. She was looking tired and unhappy.

'It was August last year,' she said. 'I was away on holiday and heard about it when I came back.'

'I was here last August.' Lorna paused, aware of some connection.

They were speaking of Etta Hood's sister. There came a sudden vivid memory of Etta's desolate cry: 'There's nobody there now but me and them.'

'What happened to Alice?' she asked.

'She drowned herself in Miller's Dam.'

It was not the time to go into details. Leaving the grim fact to speak for itself, Miss Prior shook her head unhappily and hurried off to her lodgings in the Square, unaware of the shock she had inflicted. On Lorna the effect was like that of a physical blow, immediate, direct, personal. Last August; long fair hair like silk; Miller's Dam. She had actually seen the girl, heard her wail of despair, watched her headlong flight downhill. For an instant she had felt in her own heart the pain of love rejected.

It occurred to her, awe-struck, that she had very likely been the last person to see Alice Hood alive. If only she had intervened, tried to help, called after her – 'Wait. You've left your hat.' If only she had run down, picked it up and followed her, it might not have been too late. She remembered how a cloud had moved away leaving an added brightness in the sky and on the water. The girl's slight body would scarcely ruffle its smooth surface or dull its dazzling sheen. There would be a quiet displacement of water beyond the reeds – she was such a quiet girl. Her white dress and long hair would float wide and soon grow limp. No death could be more lonely.

Rooted to the pavement where Miss Prior had left her, Lorna felt the impossibility of going home. Later she would probably hear Aunt Mabel's version of the story. It would be too trenchant, too sensible, too ordinary. On a person who had witnessed the last few minutes of Alice Hood's life the effect must be more complex. For her the drama of love and betrayal enacted on the green slope had been so compelling that she could see it still and feel, as for an instant she had felt then, something more than its physical actuality: a warning that in loving there must be pain; that love was dangerous. It was by sheer chance that she had happened to be in that solitary place at that particular moment, absurdly fanciful to imagine that because she was the only person there, the warning must be for her. Besides, there had been no need of the warning. Not then. But now. . . ? Not even now, of course.

Yet her sense of involvement in Alice Hood's fate was to persist. Already the memory of what she had seen was changing like a living thing. The remembered scene was becoming charged with menace as if a weird light effaced the sunset glow. The call of the jay seemed now a shriek threatening disaster.

She returned to reality in the shape of Victoria Terrace, its bay windows and lace curtains reassuring in their respectability – and glanced at her watch. It was not quite time for the evening meal at The Birches. A dose of Aunt Mabel would do her good but like all doses it could be postponed for a little while. For half an hour she was free to do as she liked – and not only for half an hour, she reminded herself without conviction. There were still parts of Canterlow she had not explored but she already had a favourite walk and turned back the way she had come, down Abbot's Lane to the school in the hollow and Abbot's Farm beyond.

At first her thoughts were of Etta Hood. It was hard for the girl to have to share the family disgrace. No wonder she was awkward and even hostile. Perhaps she had always taken second place to her good, nicely spoken, silken-haired elder sister whose conduct could now be resented as the cause of her own isolation from other girls – and more significantly perhaps – from boys.

From Etta she progressed to the mysterious being referred to as 'you know who'. She had felt instinctively that the other two were talking about someone connected with Mr Ushart and hinting that he had more to put up with than with the tiresome Mr Moxby. 'Nothing's changed and never will . . . Isn't it a shame?' . . . So far she had seen him as an isolated being, and with respect amounting to reverence. He had what Aunt Belle would have described as an uplifting influence. But even the most superior of human beings must have problems. When she first saw him alone at his desk, he had seemed lost in thought and not of a cheerful kind.

At the school gate she paused. The place was quiet as a precinct. Not a leaf moved. Everyone had long since gone home. Here was an opportunity to explore the garden. She went slowly up the sloping path until suddenly, with embarrassment, she found herself too close to the house. A window was closed abruptly. She had been seen – and came to her senses. It was time for her to go home too. . . .

She had been mistaken in thinking that the school was empty. In the hall two people confronted each other.

'You've missed a good many lessons, Etta. Do you want to grow up into an ignorant woman?'

'No, sir.'

'I'm glad to hear it. You're a clever girl and learn quickly. I'm glad you are with us again. What made you come back?'

'I like Miss Kent, sir.'

'Then you can please her by taking pains with your needle-work, can't you?'

'Yes, sir.'

'Run home now and have your tea.'

Behind the dutiful responses there had been no yielding to authority. She was, he knew, immovable as rock. No inner stirring had altered her expression, which a very slight contortion of feature could have made baleful. One could imagine her like Medusa turning any relationship to stone. The dead-white skin and thin crimson lips that nature had inflicted on her suggested a malignity extraordinary in so young a girl: misleading, it was to be hoped. Apart from truancy she was as yet innocent of wrong-doing so far as he knew, and she would soon be leaving the district. Besides, she was not completely heartless: she liked Miss Kent.

He watched her from the window until she disappeared into the lane. Presently he saw Lorna coming down the garden path. It was with a different expression that he watched her too until she passed out of sight.

# Chapter 6

Lorna's first impressions of the school and its setting were not dispelled as she became part of it, though always on its outer edge, so that she never experienced the total immersion that makes detachment impossible. For her the idyllic charm of the place was never quite lost.

As the days lengthened orchard trees blossomed, flowerbeds came into bloom, windows stood open to admit mild air and birdsong. The quiet hours slipped by and she was wonderfully content with only one reservation: to wish that things could continue in the same way forever could not be reconciled with a proper concern for Miss Webber's health and the hope that she would soon be well.

She had confessed as much to Mr Ushart when towards the end of term he asked her if she enjoyed her work.

'It doesn't seem like work.'

'I wonder if that's because you spend your time with the girls and in their quieter moments.'

Lorna smiled. She had seen and quailed from the savagery and uproar of the schoolyard at playtime.

'Or is it because I'm here only for a while? I might not feel so carefree if it was lifelong and inescapable.'

Had she offended him? His eyebrows had knit in a quick frown.

'Lifelong and inescapable?'

'I only meant that I come here as an outsider without having to face the difficult tiring work. I do admire Miss Prior and Miss Ellwood – and wonder if I would love it so much if I had to depend on it for my living.'

'You love it?'

She hesitated. Her feelings were too personal and remote from sober judgement to be expressed, least of all to him. She knew very well that her present happiness did not stem entirely from the girls and their needlework.

'There's nothing I'd rather do,' she said. 'But it's wrong to want things to go on just as they are now instead of hoping that Miss Webber will soon be well enough to take over.'

'You don't think one can be in two opposing states of mind at the same time – or in such quick succession that neither can be acted upon?'

He was so patient and understanding that she wondered why at first she had thought him distant. He certainly could be stern. She had heard the swish of the cane and seen red-eared boys blowing on their hands and blinking away tears. But she felt that his occasionally sombre moods were not temperamental. She thought of him as a man whom nature intended to be happy; but with a school, a wife (delicate, Miss Prior said), two children and active work on various committees to worry about it was no wonder that he sometimes seemed less than cheerful.

It was not unusual to find him waiting to speak to her at the end of the afternoon, to discuss an order for material or whether a girl could be recommended to an employer. Such details could have been dealt with in two minutes at any time in the day; but undisturbed in the empty building, he at his desk, she on a chair opposite, they would progress from the cost of calico or the fitting of a new needle-holder in the sewing-machine to wider topics. She had never really known her father, was little used to masculine company and had never before

experienced the warmth that comes from sympathetic attention
or felt such admiration as Adam Ushart's superiority of mind
roused in her, not to mention his personal charm. She felt that
he too enjoyed their brief times together though naturally they
could not be as precious to him as they had become to her.

If it had been suggested to her that it was unsuitable to spend
time alone with Mr Ushart, Lorna would have been astonished.

'But he's married,' she would have protested, amused that the
fact seemed to have been overlooked. The mores of her class
and background placed him, for that very reason, in so strongly
fortified a social group that no impropriety was possible.
Married men were not only different from other men but in
most cases uninteresting and on the whole scarcely to be
noticed. Besides, Mr Ushart was quite old, almost twice her age
and in a sense her employer. She could talk to him, even confide
in him more freely than in any man of her own age: indeed
anyone else at all.

'People like me are at a disadvantage,' she had once told him;
and when he raised his eyebrows in disbelief, 'It's true. If we had
been poor or if my father was a man who worked with his hands,
I would have been sent to the local school. I would have made
friends there and would have gone out to work when I was fourteen. If we'd been rich, I would have gone to an expensive
school. . . .'

'Where you would have learned how to behave at country
house parties.'

'There are good schools for girls. I might have been properly
educated.'

'Whereas. . . .'

'Whereas I was sent to a small private school and learned
nothing worthwhile. You must see that it's a disadvantage to
have no training, no knowledge of any depth and no skills. Since
knowing Miss Prior and the other teachers, I envy them.'

'Since knowing you,' he echoed her phrase with amusement,

'I have more respect for small private schools than ever before. As for having no knowledge of any depth, the cure is obvious. They taught you to read, didn't they?'

Books were the source of all wisdom. She must educate herself by reading. Occasionally, when the others had gone home, he would have a book for her: Stevenson's essays, Ruskin's *The Crown of Wild Olives*, a biography of Florence Nightingale. In her room at The Birches during the Easter holidays she read earnestly, pausing to think of what she would ask him, her interest in the printed word yielding perhaps too soon to mental pictures of his face, his smile, his moments of romantic gloom. Hemmed in by two wardrobes, a brace of toilet tables and a washstand, she soared into less congested realms. By the time school started again, it seemed like the resumption of an old habit to spend an occasional quarter of an hour alone with him. Nothing had changed. He remained as he had always been, pleasantly aloof. But to a person listening to him and watching him with unflagging interest, not even the smallest alteration in speech or manner could pass unnoticed.

Under his guidance she had become a little more familiar with Shakespeare's plays, especially the tragedies.

'Keep this for a while.' He had been holding a little red volume from the Arden pocket edition. '*Hamlet, Macbeth* and *Othello* between two covers. Dip into them from time to time. It would take you the rest of your life to know them well.'

She had stayed longer than usual, long enough to be conscious of the time and had already gone to the door. She turned. He was still flicking through the pages. As she came back, he half turned away, ripped out a double page and crammed it in the pocket of his jacket, then put the book in her outstretched hand, disregarding any surprise she might have shown. Indeed she was surprised but his own lack of comment made it impossible for her to remark on it.

The small incident was memorable. It was as if a crack had

opened in his smooth self-containment. One didn't tear a page out of any book, least of all a double page from a Shakespearean play, except for some good reason. The west-facing window was full of sunlight. She was blinded by it and could not see his face as he turned to his desk as if waiting for her to go so that he could sit down. That he was put out in some way was so obvious that she felt embarrassed for him. Lest he should think she had noticed his change of manner, she murmured thanks and left rather abruptly.

Pondering the incident in her own room, she continued to find it strange. It was her habit of mind to remember events pictorially so that whenever she opened the book – and that was often if only because he had told her to – she recalled, like the scene in a glass paperweight, the shaft of sunlight in which he had stood, his tall figure dark against the window so that at first she saw only his left hand holding the red book and his right hand reaching over to rip out the page; then, as she moved out of the light, she saw his sudden frown.

Something had caught his eye: a word, a line, a situation; something familiar – a reminder of some other occasion perhaps when it, whatever it was, had provoked him. Even the reminder of it had provoked him again to the point of forgetting that he was not alone. But why tear it out – unless it was something he didn't want her to read? She turned the pages thoughtfully and was to do so many times. There must be a gap in the text where the missing double page had been. Having found the place, she had only to find the passage in Uncle Arthur's *Complete Works of Shakespeare* to read the offending lines. That it would be an act of vulgar curiosity did not deter her: vulgarly curious she undoubtedly was, sufficiently so to make quite a hobby of it. But the research involved her in careful reading if not of every word, certainly of the last line on every page and the first line on the next. The sheer tedium of it defeated her. The search was abandoned; Uncle Arthur's weighty volume resumed its long repose and gradually the incident faded from her mind.

# Chapter 7

There was nothing remarkable in the fact that so far she had not met or even seen Mrs Ushart. The schoolhouse at the top of the garden was of the same period as the older part of the school, with small-paned windows mullioned and transomed in stone. Access to the garden was from a side door. The front door opened on the street so that comings and goings were not seen from the school. Mrs Ushart took no part in local affairs: she was often ill and with young children, she had, it was agreed, enough on her plate.

Lorna had dismissed her class one afternoon and stayed behind to undo some hopelessly crooked seams when she heard footsteps in the entrance and an agitated voice.

'Can somebody come – quick?'

In the hall a young woman with lank untidy hair and wearing a dirty apron was looking round wildly.

'Oh miss, can you please come? Mrs Ushart's taken real bad and there's nobody to see to little Paul and Amy while I run for the doctor if he's there which he might not be. The master won't be home till seven o'clock. He's gone to a meeting in Gorsham. Everything's in a mess.' For all her anxiety the girl hesitated when they arrived at the side door. 'Between her and the children I've had no chance to clear up. Be careful, miss.'

Lorna groped her way along a dark passage, avoiding a pail

and scrubbing brush, a basket of soiled linen and a burnt saucepan soaking in soapy water, to a room opening off the hall.

One glance round what must be the family living-room was enough to affront every housewifely instinct encouraged in her by her aunts. Mrs Ushart was lying on the sofa. Of all that was memorable in that first meeting – the sickly smell, the blood-stained rags, an enamel bowl full of some nauseously slimy fluid – of all that demanded attention, her first impression, true, lasting, never to change, was of Madeline Ushart's face.

It was turned towards her, deathly pale against the shabby green of the sofa. It expressed neither interest nor any appeal for help. It seemed a mask of suffering and at the same time, against all likelihood, a mask of extraordinary beauty. There could be no circumstance in life – no illness, no unhappiness – in which it would be other than beautiful. In death it would have the same sculpturesque dignity. Black hair, blue eyes and perfection of feature had no need of the charm that comes from vitality.

But on the threshold of the disordered room, after the first dazzling glimpse, Lorna had no time to analyse, admire or envy. As the blue eyes closed again under heavy lids, she thought the worst had happened and that she was looking at a beautiful corpse. At the same time she discovered to her dismay that the two children were also in the room. From behind a pedestal table with a cloth of green plush rose two heads, those of a six-year-old boy and his younger sister.

'Paul?'

He stood up.

'Mother has been ill.' He spoke with the firm clarity of an adult. 'Tilly didn't know what to do.'

'Have you come to make her well again?' Amy peered anxiously over the green cloth. Both remained staunchly in the narrow space between table and wall as in a stronghold against encroaching disaster.

Feeling no less uncertain than Tilly as to what to do, Lorna

bent over their mother and touched her hand. To her relief the
eyes opened.

'What can I do for you, Mrs Ushart?'

A slight shake of the head, a hand pointing to the blanket
covering the lower part of her body. Lorna raised it. There had
been a heavy discharge of blood.

'Paul. Has your father any brandy?'

'It's in the sideboard. Shall I fetch a spoon?'

'Yes, please. And you and Amy need not stay.'

'We sometimes sit on the stairs,' Amy told her. 'Shall we go and
sit on the stairs?'

'How good the children are!' Lorna said as they tiptoed away.

For the first time their mother showed some faint consciousness of her plight – and theirs. Her eyes filled. Her lips moved.
Lorna leaned closer.

'They're used to my misery.' The weak whisper faded.

In the kitchen Lorna found a kettle on the hob and after
rummaging for a clean towel and basin, bathed the invalid's face,
neck and hands.

'You're very kind.' The brandy had revived her. 'Who are you?'

'Let me stay with you until the doctor comes.'

A nod, a softening of the lips, a faint smile as she sank back
exhausted. Minutes crept by. . . . Lorna itched to do something
about the room but hesitated to disturb Mrs Ushart or remove the
evidence of her condition before the doctor came. She could at
least clear the small table by the sofa of the remains of an uneaten
breakfast and a pot of tea brewed hours ago. In the kitchen there
were dishes to be washed. She stoked the fire, filled the kettle and
put it on the cross-bar; and all the time, more urgent even than
her concern for the woman was the conviction that her husband
must never know that an outsider, to some extent a member of his
staff, had intruded on a situation so – it was hard to define –
discreditable to his position? Wounding to his dignity? Squalid?
Of the squalor at least there could be no doubt.

She was in the kitchen when Tilly came back, followed almost at once by the doctor and Mrs Foxon, the local nurse and midwife, whom she took to the living-room. When she came back to the kitchen, Lorna closed the door.

'They haven't seen me. I'd rather they didn't know I'm here. Let me do that.' Tilly had started to cut bread and butter for the children. Lorna took the knife and made her sit down.

'This will do for your tea. You've had a bad time. When you're feeling better you can take the children to Mrs Hobcroft at The Birches. I would take them myself but they'd be sure to tell their father and I particularly don't want him to know that a stranger has intruded on his home. With the children out of the way you can catch up with some of your work.'

'Such as I've been trying to do since goodness knows when. The geyser has gone wrong again. It has to be a kettle every time I need hot water.'

'I'll bring them back and they can be in bed when he comes home. Seven o'clock, you said. Naturally they'll tell him where they've been. You can say that you came to school for help and that I told you to take them to Mrs Hobcroft's.'

The plan was unsatisfactory but by this time she was more than ever convinced that he would dislike having the wretched state of his home known. That it was not known throughout Canterlow, astonishing as that was, signified how careful he had been to protect his privacy. She gave only a guarded account of Mrs Ushart's situation to Aunt Mabel and tried to restrain her in the days to come from sending too much food to the stricken household.

'There's a lot for one girl to do, with an invalid into the bargain,' her aunt observed when Tilly had brought the children and hurried off. 'They could do with more help. He has £110 a year and the house, but doctor's bills can run away with a lot of money. I did hear that she comes from a well-to-do family but she doesn't seem to be doing too well now, poor thing.'

The children enjoyed their visit, especially their tea.

'This is a splendid house.' Paul gazed wide-eyed at the splendour of the Hobcroft dining-room with its well-worn, well-polished furniture and well-tended pot-plants; its pink lustres on the sideboard and white chair-backs of crocheted lace – and endeared himself for ever to his hostess.

'Such a polite, sensitive child. He's like his father. If he does as much good in the world as Mr Ushart does, his mother will be proud of him. If she lives to see it. It's a pity we couldn't wash their clothes but they'd never have been dry in time.'

Nevertheless, fed, bathed, their hair brushed and shoes polished, they were a handsome pair when at six o'clock Lorna was ready to take them home. Fortunately – she was becoming obsessed by the need to prevent gossip – their own maid Gladys was having her afternoon off. Amy climbed on Aunt Mabel's knee and kissed her with a confidence and enthusiasm Lorna had been incapable of at a similar age.

Despite her contriving, the plan to efface herself completely out of respect for his feelings was almost ruined by Mr Ushart's too early return. As she took the children quietly across the hall on their way to bed, she glanced into the living room. Their mother was still on the sofa but her husband was now at her side. She saw them only for a moment, just long enough to see him smooth his wife's hair from her brow and to see her turn her head away from him and push his hand aside.

'It looks as if it'll be the cottage hospital again.' Tilly was in the children's bedroom, getting out clean night things in honour of Miss Kent.

'Again?'

'It's never ending, miss, the sickness and misery in this house. She's never been right since Amy was born, neither in body nor in her spirits.'

The girl was worn out and had spoken out of turn, but she had also spoken from the heart and Lorna believed her. The word 'misery' twice used, dismayed her. She went quickly downstairs and let herself out by the garden door. It was pleasant to be alone under the trees; to breathe fresh air faintly wallflower-scented and hear the church clock impartially striking the half-hour. And out of doors it was still day-light. How dark the rooms had been with their small windows in need of a good clean! How quiet the children had been, shut away upstairs! They had been quiet all day. Of course the circumstances had been distressing: their mother was obviously a very sick woman; worse still, she seemed utterly weary of life as if she had lost interest in everything that should have made it worth living, even her family. She had seemed to shrink from the touch of her husband's hand. He would understand that it was a sign of her condition but it must have grieved him: he was so sensitive, so considerate of others.

Her own respect for him softened into sympathy bordering – it would have been undreamed of until then – on pity. The object of her admiration and respect was after all, she conceded, a human being. Any man would be saddened by the lack of the loving support that he of all men so richly deserved. Unconsciously her manner towards him changed. Glimpses of his home life had made him even more interesting. Knowing his difficulties, she rose a little nearer to his own level and felt less in awe of him. A touch of protectiveness crept into her attitude, softened her voice and gave her an added sweetness, a charm she was unaware of.

As for the crisis at the schoolhouse, if there was gossip about the Usharts among the ladies of Canterlow, she was unaware of that too. Had they known of them, they would have been more interested in the deplorable domestic arrangements than in Mrs Ushart's condition. Miscarriages were not uncommon and the poor woman was always unwell in one way or another. Aunt Mabel's comment that one might expect a man in his position to be more considerate was made to Lorna alone. As a school manager she would have felt it unbecoming to criticize the headmaster especially as there was so very much to be said in his favour.

Some weeks later it was rumoured that a relative had come from Scotland to act as temporary housekeeper: a widow, Mrs McNab. The news was received with approval: it was to be hoped that she would stay. In Miss Prior's opinion the headmaster would be none the worse for having regular well-cooked meals. Paul, in the infant class, had perked up, Miss Ellwood said, and arrived at school every morning fortified by porridge for breakfast and wearing a clean jersey twice a week.

Though Mrs Ushart was often in her thoughts – that is in such thoughts as could be spared from Mr Ushart – Lorna had not seen her again and there seemed no reason why they should ever meet. To think of her was to remember how tenderly – or was it tentatively – he had stroked her hair, to feel ashamed of remembering, and depressed. But one afternoon he waylaid her as she was going home and this time it was not of books that he wanted to talk.

'Would it be too much, Miss Kent, to ask you to do me a favour?'

Could there be anything in the world she would not do for him? The extravagance of her thoughts could perhaps be excused since there could be no outlet for her feelings.

'It's about my wife. I fancy it may have been you who persuaded Mrs Hobcroft to have the children in May?'

'Aunt Mabel needed no persuasion. She was glad to be able to help.'

'You are both very kind. Otherwise I wouldn't ask. . . .' He was not quite at ease. 'Dr Bordman feels that she needs more company. Congenial company. Mrs McNab is a very sensible woman but she isn't . . . she hasn't time for the sort of companionship my wife needs. Would you . . . could you bear to call occasionally and keep her company for half an hour or so from time to time? She is on her own all day. . . .'

So began a series of rather cautious meetings leading to something like friendship with Madeline Ushart. Lorna called next morning and found her as before – unable to leave the sofa but otherwise improved in health.

'So – you are Miss Kent. When my husband mentioned your name I was at a loss. But you came, didn't you, when I was ill? Like a little ghost appearing and disappearing.'

It took a moment or two to adjust to the change. When last seen she had seemed barely alive. Her manner was now confident.

'You were very ill and only half-conscious at the time, Mrs Ushart, otherwise you wouldn't have taken me for a ghost.'

'Then give me your hand so that I can be sure you're real.'

They talked about the children. Amy came to say How-do-you-do and show off a new pinafore, then crept to the hiding-place behind the table to play with her doll.

'You haven't regretted leaving town?'

'I wouldn't have been happy there without Aunt Belle.'

'And there was no one else you were sorry to leave?'

The implication of the question was obvious. Lorna disregarded it.

'Friends, of course.'

'And your parents?'

It was undemanding talk suited to the needs of an invalid. Had its flow run dry there would have remained the pleasure of looking at her. How lovely she must have been as a bride! How deeply he must love her!

It was not long before they became Lorna and Madeline, always alone together except when Mrs McNab brought a tray of tea. She was a middle-aged woman, pleasant to look at and becomingly though plainly dressed. Mr Ushart's reference to her had been rather dismissive. In fact he might have searched the length and breadth of the land for a housekeeper without finding her equal. Moreover she was obviously disinclined to waste time in idle talk and always left Lorna to pour out.

As time went on the very act of presiding over the teapot enhanced the feeling of being almost though never quite at home. She did realize that the developing friendship should be good for her as well as for the invalid, with its constant reminders that the only man she had ever been interested in was Madeline's husband. That was all it was, naturally: an interesting friendship. Between her and his wife no intimate confidences were exchanged. It was impossible to discover whether the rejection of her husband's soothing hand had been the fretful recoil of an exhausted woman or whether he really was more loving than loved. What could not be in doubt was that it was no business of hers.

On the whole their conversation was impersonal talk kept going simply out of politeness, without the intervals of companionable silence that punctuate sympathetic exchanges – or so it seemed. Yet an eavesdropper on the woman's casual questions and the girl's brief answers might have been aware that Mrs Ushart learned a good deal about Lorna, her history and temperament, whereas Lorna learned next to nothing about her hostess.

'You and your aunt were close companions?'

'Very close.' Lorna's voice was not quite steady.

'It would have been different if she had married, I suppose.'

'I suppose it would.'

'Perhaps she had lost someone in the war. So many women did.'

'I don't think so.'

If there had been a romantic attachment, as surely there must have been, Aunt Belle had never mentioned it. It must have been the one avenue they had never explored. As a little girl she had sometimes asked why Aunt Belle had no husband. The questions were ignored or said to be rude, like asking a person's age, and she had come to realize that the topic was unwelcome – which meant that there had been someone. Someday perhaps she might have been confided in. Mr Liffey had had a younger brother who died of enteric fever. . . .

'Well, some women are not successful in finding husbands – or don't want to be. And yet sometimes shy, withdrawn women make excellent wives.'

'Oh, Aunt Belle wasn't like that. She was very sociable. Everyone liked her.'

'You had quite a circle?'

There were the Liffeys, she was told. Rita Liffey was engaged to Maurice Denby, who had a leg wound. They would soon be getting married. Like the Liffeys the Denbys were well established in business, and there were the Wilburs, especially Faith.

In enlarging on what Madeline described as her circle in Donnerton, Lorna had the curious experience of discovering things she had never previously known – or given thought to. She rather enjoyed it. Seen from a distance the characters were purged of imperfections that had sometimes been tiresome at close quarters. Warming to the subject, she managed to convey with an approval she had never been called upon to show, a way of life she had taken for granted. It had been a good life, without glamour, without mystery. People spoke their minds and if there was nothing remarkable in what was said, neither was there any deception. Apart from her aunt's reluctance to dwell on a possible disappointment in love, there was nothing for the Featherstones or Liffeys or Denbys to conceal, so far as she knew. As for the Wilburs, Faith's yea was yea and her nay was nay without qualification.

Once or twice, with a sudden change of mood, she felt the contrast in her present surroundings. The impression of concealment was probably due in part to the actual setting: the gloom, the faded colours, the dark corners and creaking doors. When they were closed against the homely clank of saucepans and the rattle of pots in the kitchen, the silence between thick walls could be felt as having actual weight like a thick pall.

The woman in the other chair was pallid, the pallor faintly luminous. Sometimes she seemed momentarily unreal as if the dusk of the room would thicken and enclose her until the last pale glimmer of her face faded and she became another dark shape among the thronging shadows.

As the summer holidays approached, Lorna steeled herself to accept a polite intimation that her supervision of the needlework would no longer be required. When her connection with the school ended, she would have no further contact with the master. Her visits to the schoolhouse might continue for a while until Madeline no longer needed or wanted her. Until then to sit in his house without seeing him, to be with his wife and never hear him mentioned could only intensify the hope that at any minute he would appear, until against her will the hope became a longing. The thought came with a pang that startled her. He had become more important to her than she had realized: more important than was right.

'I shall never be well again, you know,' Madeline said one day, changing the subject of their somewhat idle talk with an unusual abruptness. Her manner as a rule was unemphatic with the smoothness of good breeding. 'Physically I'm useless. In every respect.'

It was not a remark to which an immediate answer sprang to the lips.

'You're better than you were,' Lorna said at last. 'And how can you be useless when you have the children?' She spoke sincerely, unconscious of her glaring omission.

'The children. Yes, of course.'

Blue eyes and grey were evenly matched. Whether Lorna knew it or not Madeline was accustomed to looking at her as constantly as she herself was looked at. Now her attention had sharpened.

'Amy will start school next year.' Lorna's intention was simply to continue a subject of interest to them both.

'And then he'll have both of them.'

If it was the tentative opening of a secret door, she closed it again at once and lay back as though weary. Lorna took the hint and left. Physically Madeline might be as useless as she was beautiful, but the acquaintance begun when Lorna came to her rescue had subtly changed. To be useless was not to be helpless. She knew that when Madeline wished to put an end to her visits she would end them without hesitation and without regret. The delicate creature she had found close to death was stronger than might have been expected. It was even possible that the dominant force in the schoolhouse was not the headmaster.

# Chapter 8

A warm day in late June brought an unexpected visitor.

'It's a gentleman asking for you, ma'am.' Gladys had been banished to 'do' the bedrooms while Mrs Hobcroft made raspberry jam. Not that she minded getting out of the kitchen for a change except that it was no better than torture doing Miss Lorna's room. Manoeuvring the sweeper round all that furniture, most of it too heavy to move, needed one of them contortionists.

'That will be the man from the Oakwood Insurance. Give this a stir.' Aunt Mabel handed Lorna the wooden spoon. 'And for mercy's sake don't let it boil over.' She was gone but only for a minute.

'Well, what do you think? It's Cedric Liffey. You go and talk to him.'

He was waiting in the sitting-room and came forward, to take her hand.

'Cedric! It's good to see you.'

'I wasn't sure if I should. . . . I mean, whether you would. . . . But it seemed a pity not to call.' He was on his way to Gorsham. to see about an order. The train stopped at Canterlow and he thought. . . . He just wanted to. . . .

'I'm glad you did. Do sit down. You look well.'

He had lost weight and in his formal business clothes was no longer the unimpressive, tongue-tied Cedric she had known ever since they were partners for the polka at Miss Terence's dancing class in the Shakespeare Hall when they were ten and twelve years old; nor the bewildered Cedric recently out of khaki. She was genuinely pleased to see him. They became immersed in news of Donnerton. She wanted to hear about Rita and Faith. Gladys was recalled from upstairs to see to the jam and Aunt Mabel joined them to ask about old friends. After all she had been born and bred in Donnerton. He must stay for lunch.

But his appointment in Gorsham at three o'clock made that impossible, he was sorry to say, seated stiffly with his capable craftsman's hands on his pinstriped trouser-knees. He could have taken a train that went straight through Canterlow without stopping or for that matter settled the bit of business by post. To call uninvited had taken courage of a calibre different from but little less desperate than that required for going over the top into enemy gunfire.

Aunt Mabel's enquiries being more penetrating than Lorna's, it was discovered that Cedric was now a full partner in the family business which was doing well. Donnerton had prospered, thanks to the recent demand for guns and bayonets. Now the cutlers and silversmiths were coming into their own again.

The call was, of necessity, short. There was just time for sandwiches and coffee before he caught the next train to Gorsham. Lorna walked with him to the station and was able to hear more about the new crèche Faith had established in Brandon, one of the lower parts of the city in every sense.

'It's not a bad little place, Canterlow.' From the platform Cedric saw the ruined castle on its eminence above roofs and tops of trees bordering the Beam. 'I wouldn't have minded seeing a little more of it.'

The silence into which might have been dropped an invitation to come again remained unbroken until the thunder of his approaching train brought the visit to an end.

'Do give my love to your mother and Rita.'

'And don't forget – mother would like you to come and stay for a few days if ever you feel like it.'

'How kind of her. One of these days. . . .'

He took off his hat as they shook hands, put it on again, climbed aboard and lowered the window for a last look at her.

'Goodbye, Lorna.'

His voice was deep and rather loud. It would have needed to be deeper and louder still to reach her in the preoccupation that held her remote from every man in the world but one. She had returned to the dangerous languor of dreaming of him before the red light at the rear of the train had passed out of sight.

'I hear the Hoods are leaving at last.' Aunt Mabel, returning from a morning call in Raven Terrace, had seen a furniture wagon at their door. 'It's to be hoped things will turn out better for them, wherever they're going.'

Lorna had never mentioned the Hoods, nor until then had her aunt. The scandal had died down by the time she came to The Birches. In time, no doubt on some evening of fireside talk, it would have featured in Aunt Mabel's repertoire of sensational events, as had the story of Will Gainfree's attempt to kill his wife with a butcher's cleaver or the happier tale of the missing five-year-old found unharmed at the bottom of a disused well. So far it had not done so.

For Lorna, simply hearing the name was enough to revive the peculiar sense of involvement she had felt in Alice Hood's situation even before she knew of its dreadful end: a mingling of sympathy and foreboding too irrational to share, especially with Aunt Mabel. But she had given little thought to the stricken family. She could never forget Etta's desolate cry: 'There's nobody now, only me and them', and had thought of the girl as strange and unapproachable without fully realizing that she was sad and lonely.

Her return to school had been puzzling. She sat in the back row, speaking to no one, with a piece of untouched needlework in front of her; but she did listen, elbows on the table, hands clasping her face, when Lorna read aloud in the quarter of an hour's story time. What she made of the blameless characters in *A Peep Behind the Scenes* and *Little Women* there was no knowing. Their gentle pathos may not have moved a girl who had seen into the abyss of human misery. But she was no trouble.

Sometimes as Lorna walked home, she was aware of Etta close behind and walked more slowly to let her catch up but she never did. She had left school at Easter and Lorna had not seen her since then. Now, roused to regret for not having been kinder, she could at least make an effort to see her again and say goodbye.

A wagon with two great shire horses blocked the road. The house door stood wide. Two men were manoeuvring a sideboard along the passage. She waited until they reached the wagon, then went to the door and called: 'Etta! Are you there?'

She appeared and came slowly along the passage. It was a relief in a way to see that she had been crying, but distressing too. Her hair hung loose about her face and halfway down her back. With a pang of *déja-vu* Lorna saw that it was no longer mousy in colour but was turning fairer, here and there brightening into gold.

'I came to say goodbye, Etta.'

The girl's eyes under reddened lids were void of warmth and so lacking in communication that she seemed to be looking through and beyond her visitor. Whatever it was she saw, it isolated her.

'I brought you a little keepsake to remember me by.' In a hasty rummaging in her drawer she had come upon a brooch of thin ivory shaped like a cameo and carved to represent a female figure under a weeping willow. Etta took it, glanced at it, then raised her head and looked longer at the giver.

'I'll remember you,' she said and Lorna felt ashamed. Parting with the brooch meant nothing to her: she had never liked it.

Behind them one of the horses stamped an immense hoof and breathed a tremendous sigh.

'I hope you'll like living in London. You'll be starting a new life,' she said and stood aside as the removal men came purposefully up the path again.

There seemed nothing else to say. She turned away, was halfway to the gate—

'But we'll be leaving her here all by herself.'

It was a lamentation. The tone and sudden overflow of feeling raised the words above the level of ordinary speech to a grief-stricken cry that must surely linger in the air as it would linger in memory. It came from a broken heart. That was it. When Alice Hood's heart was broken, her sister's heart broke too. With a gush of pity Lorna turned to hurry back, put her arms round the girl and try to comfort her. It was too late: Etta had gone, leaving her to feel once more the regret that comes from having failed to act – or speak – while there was still time.

Crossing the bridge on her way home, she remembered the king-fisher, only to forget it as she looked down at the water and tried to imagine what it must be like to drown. The Beam flowed less swiftly than on the March day when she had first seen Etta, but its current was strong in midstream, an active force indifferent to everything but its own inscrutable purpose. In contrast the smooth water of Miller's Dam might seem to offer a kindlier resting-place.

Half an hour later she stood on its southern bank. It was almost a year since she had looked down on it from the ridge on the other side. This time she had come through the churchyard, a shorter way. The uncut meadows on either side of the water were deep in flowering grasses, sorrel, clover and moon daisies. Last August they had been greening again after the hay harvest. There had been no tall flower stems then for Alice to tread down as she went headlong to her death.

Today the sun was warm, the air sweet. How could one bear to leave it – forever? How had she dared to leave the known world, however cruel, and risk what was to come? Would she, Lorna Kent, finding herself in such a predicament, choose to die? Dread of disgrace must surely be less awesome than ceasing to exist at all. Perhaps it was not fear of public humiliation that drove Alice to her death. No humiliation could be more wounding than that she had already suffered as she slid to the ground at her lover's feet and lay face down, weeping as he walked away.

So far Lorna had given little thought to the man. He was vile of course, no better than a murderer: she had consigned him to the more severe torments of the damned. But her memory of the incident had been visual. She had seen it from above, framed in arching branches, its colours gold and white and green: the sloping green hillside, the golden light, the white figure of the girl lying abandoned – a sacrifice to unhallowed love, she had afterwards thought – and no one else. The man had walked out of the picture.

But now, from this lower point and on the other side of the water, she could reconstruct the scene in reverse. All that remained of an ancient hedge between the meadow and the pasture above it were a few straggling hawthorns. They had shaded a few yards of the path at the eastern end where the lovers had stood and had partially screened the man. From this side of the dam she would have seen him completely, the hawthorns no longer serving as a screen but as a backcloth to his whole figure. Thinking in this way gave him physical reality: he existed. More than that: not only was she herself the last person to have seen Alice Hood alive; she was the only person so far as she knew to have come within minutes of identifying the man Alice had so unwisely loved.

How easy simply to walk away! How far had he gone? What distance had he thought fit to put between himself and the girl whose life he had blighted and the child she might have borne?

Who was he? The need to know was not a matter of idle curiosity, rather of concern, combined with a revival of her strange feeling of kinship with Alice Hood. It seemed a kind of obligation to find out who he was and force him to answer for the harm he had done. Wherever else he might be, he had invaded her mind. And if she did find out more about him, what earthly good would it do? It would serve no useful purpose. The Hoods had gone: she was unlikely to see or hear of them again; the parents remained a mysterious They and Them whom she had never seen. As for Etta, to hark back to the tragedy would very likely aggravate a nervous or mental sickness which only time and absence from Canterlow could heal.

Yet having got the man into her mind she could not get him out of it. It had already become a habit to take long walks. At first they were a necessary escape from The Birches, where the privacy of her own room had to be shared with too much furniture and the living-rooms with Aunt Mabel. But it had soon become deeply satisfying to discover high-banked green lanes and bridle paths for centuries unchanged. The richness of the soil and the softness of the air combined to drape the hedgerows with honeysuckle, elder blossom and wild roses and crowd the waysides with flowers. The atmosphere in summer was conducive to submission rather than action. It stimulated the inner life. Half an hour's walk could induce imaginative activity so absorbing that it was easy to lose touch with such things as hard facts.

For most of the time one theme had occupied her mind when she was alone. There could be nothing wrong in it: nothing wrong in so one-sided a friendship when the other person had no idea that it existed. Friendship was all it was, though different from any other she had known, she told herself, ignoring or trying to ignore the nature of the difference: the delight she felt in seeing him, the quickened heartbeat when he smiled at her.

Even if it was more than friendship, could there be anything wrong in loving when no one knew of it, least of all himself; when

71

no one was made unhappy by it; when she gave no sign, content to be alone to think of him? In Donnerton such a state of mind, rapturous and exalted, could not have survived the company of friends and the various activities which had once filled her days. But here there was little to discourage dreaming, particularly by the dam in the valley of the Beam where she had first become aware – too vividly – of the danger of loving.

From the day when she let Etta go without trying to comfort her, thoughts of the Hoods occasionally troubled her with a feeling of guilt until gradually her thoughts of Alice Hood's ill-fated love became entwined with thoughts of her own situation. Were they alike? In her own case there was as yet nothing to regret except the folly of thinking too much about a man beyond her reach. But if she had been in Alice's place and similar demands had been made on her. . . ? Even to imagine those demands, however vaguely, brought a thrill more piercing than any friendship could rouse. It was a revelation. No one could save Alice, but Alice by her example might be the means of saving her. In those poignant moments when they had been alone together on the green hillside, she had learned that there can be pain in loving but she had not realized then that the love she was witnessing was of a special kind: forbidden and unsanctified. Like her own?

The very thought could, in her saner moments, be dismissed as too far-fetched and certainly too uncomfortable to dwell on. There was no similarity whatever between herself and Alice Hood and nothing she needed to be warned against. . . .

'I suppose you know that the Hoods have left.' She had met Miss Prior outside the library one Saturday morning and invited her to coffee in the Beamside Tea-Room. 'Do you think Etta will ever get over her sister's death?'

'She's young – and she'll feel better in a place where there's nothing to remind her of it.'

'You're probably right.' Lorna stirred her coffee. 'It's not a pleasant thought but I suppose he could be walking about in Canterlow this very minute as if nothing had happened.'

'He? Oh, you mean the man, whoever he is.'

'Who *is* he? Someone must know.'

Apparently not. Submitting to half an hour of leisure before taking the Girl Guides on a picnic, Miss Prior was not averse to passing on all that she knew of the town gossip at the time of the tragedy. Interest had been revived by the Hoods' departure. Since no one knew who the seducer was, the field of conjecture might have been wider if any other girl had been his victim; but Alice was different, a quiet, pious girl innocent of even a flirtation with any of the local boys. Suspicion had rested briefly on Ben Salton, stableman at the Duke's Arms, a rough wild young man, whom the girls of Canterlow were warned against. 'He's just the type,' Miss Prior said. But nobody seriously believed that Alice Hood, a Sunday School teacher, refined and modest in her ways, would so much as pass the time of day with red-faced, beer-drinking Ben. Besides if it had been a local lad there would have been no scandal. The Hoods would perforce have accepted any decent husband – any husband at all – for a daughter who had behaved as Alice had done.

'Then I suppose it must have been a stranger.'

An outsider: someone unknown in Canterlow? A year ago the war was still going on. There had been all sorts of comings and goings in wartime.

'Well, yes.' Miss Prior looked round and lowered her voice to a whisper. It was evidently on this one point that tongues had wagged more discreetly though with even greater disapproval.

There had been a very pleasant young man, a lay preacher from Gorsham way. He had been seen in Canterlow more often than he had preached there, before leaving for the mission field in China: a well-spoken young man, very correct.

'Or seemed to be,' Miss Prior concluded, fishing in her purse for a sixpence.

'No, no. You're my guest.'

'It's been very nice. Just pray that it stays fine fill five o'clock. After that it doesn't matter.'

Lorna poured out another cup of coffee and drank it slowly, revising on more definite lines her mental image of Alice's lover, than which nothing could be vaguer. The pleasant young preacher would naturally be wearing black: it was a Sunday. He might have been preaching at Canterlow that day – and for the last time. The pleasant young hypocrite, she thought scathingly, and pictured Alice sitting through the sermon, racked with anxiety and the need to speak to him alone, while he mouthed his pleasant platitudes. Afterwards they would meet; she would tell him of her plight; he would protest that there was nothing he could do: it was his duty to fulfil a Christian mission overseas. How could he pledge himself to her, a simple country girl seventeen years old, when he was already pledged to teeming millions of pagans in China?

Fiddlesticks! He was thinking of his own reputation, indifferent to hers. There were practical ways short of marriage in which he could have helped her. Besides his nauseating hypocrisy and depravity, there must have been a streak of downright cruelty in his nature, simply to walk away. He would never know the outcome of his backsliding and could never be brought to repentance. . . .

'Who is preaching tomorrow?' She paused at the foot of the stairs as her aunt crossed the hall.

'It's one of our own lay preachers, old Mr Evans. You'll like him. His sermons are as good as you would hear anywhere.'

'I won't be going. I've been thinking things over. In future I shan't go unless one of the ministers is taking the service. Men who have pledged their lives to serving their own countrymen,' she added, 'are more likely to be worth listening to.'

'Well! I don't know what you can have against lay preachers.' Aunt Mabel raised her voice as her niece went upstairs. 'We used to have a young man from near Gorsham who was an inspiration to listen to. Everybody liked him even if he was brought up a Primitive. But he's gone. . . .'

'To China. Yes. I've heard of him.' Lorna closed her bedroom door. Her contributions to the Christian Mission Overseas would henceforth be diverted to Widows and Orphans. The unconverted Chinese would neither know nor care. Better to be a pagan, she thought, unconsciously echoing a great poet and with some confusion of metaphors, than a lustful whited sepulchre.

# Chapter 9

'It's no good, Lorna, I won't be going back.' For a moment Nora Webber's courage failed. Her light voice had hardened in despair. 'Not to school, I mean. They'll have to get somebody else.'

They were marooned amid empty beds in the deserted ward. All the windows were open. It was cold. The other patients were on the veranda where it must be colder still. Even to think of the comfortable warmth of life at The Birches seemed an affront, its cosiness shameful, her own misguided love no more than heartless self-indulgence.

The situation was too grim for any kind of soothing claptrap.

'The children have missed you.'

'Really? Do you think so?' Nora's face lit up. 'Not half as much as I've missed them.' Miss Prior was keeping her up to date with news but she was always eager for more. 'You go to see Mrs Ushart, don't you? What is she really like?'

Difficult to answer. What was she really like?

'Never well, I'm afraid. Always beautiful.'

'There now. How does she manage that? When you're ill you have to let things go.'

'That hasn't happened to you.'

The immaculate purity of Nora's surroundings seemed to have

got itself into her face. It was thin and colourless but open and endearingly without guile. Could the contrast between her and the enigmatic Madeline derive from the difference in their surroundings – between the clinical bareness of the ward and the dim rooms of an old house over-shadowed by trees, where more was left unsaid than could be shared?

'And what about Roy Moxby? As hopeless as ever, I suppose. I always had a soft spot for Roy. He should never have gone in for teaching although goodness knows what else he could have done. He was pushed into it. Yes, he's been under his stepfather's thumb most of his life. You'll know him. Councillor Garson.'

Lorna had heard of him. One couldn't help hearing of a man so active in public life and said to be on eleven committees.

'It's lucky for Roy that he's got Mr Ushart as his headmaster. No one else would put up with him.'

'What exactly is wrong with him?'

'Temperament, I suppose. He's as weak as water, I should think. There was a time – it would be about a year ago – when he seemed to go all to pieces. He's the sort –' Nora paused '– I shouldn't say it because it's a thing to be sacked for and I don't say he's taken to it but he's the sort that might. . . .'

'Drink?'

'Once or twice he's turned up looking as if he'd been out all night and didn't know what he was doing or where he should be.'

Lorna remembered the exercise books scattered in the dust, but she also remembered his anxious smile as he thanked her for helping to pick them up and his general air of finding life too difficult to cope with.

'He needs a friend. Someone to take him in hand. You might take him on, Lorna, and lick him into shape.'

They laughed. The visit ended on a cheerful note.

'I do love to see you coming down the ward. And the flowers are so beautiful. There's nothing like roses.'

Nora was still in the sanatorium when the six months of her

sick leave ended. A new teacher was appointed and Lorna's services were no longer required. She had however made a niche for herself and unofficially, as a friend of the school, kept in touch. Her help was welcomed when costumes were needed for the school concert. On Sports Day she presided over the tea-urn.

Devising costumes for Captain Hook and his pirates and wings for Peter Pan was all very well: she enjoyed it but it was no substitute for the hours spent each week in the end classroom no more than a few steps from the desk in the hall, or for chance meetings when everyone else had gone home. As time went by they had become more frequent, the exchange of ideas more warmly sympathetic. Awareness of all that must not be said had its own power to thrill, as into the decorum of so restrained a companionship crept a hint of the illicit.

When she was left more to her own devices the friendship with Madeline, with all its reservations, had continued and by virtue of its continuity, if for no other reason, had strengthened. Each would have felt it a loss if it were to end. Neither felt in it the warmth of real friendship such as Lorna had come to feel for Nora Webber and for unassuming, self-forgetful Miss Prior. But she was made welcome by Paul and Amy as well as by their mother and loved them for their own sake as well as for their father's. She saw him only as he came and went. Such brief encounters – he on his way to his study, she crossing the hall to let herself out by the side door – were enough to send her home in a mood uplifted and withdrawn, to seek the privacy of her own room for all its drawbacks. One could not describe them as shortcomings when so very many things had come there.

'Tea's ready. Aren't you ever coming down?' Aunt Mabel would call, seeing her niece's absence simply as a failure to come downstairs. How could she know that it would be a descent from the clouds?

She did in time begin to feel more strongly than ever that Lorna was not quite the girl she had taken her for. She talked less and thought more than was altogether healthy. But she was a Kent and she, Mabel, had always suspected that Bernard Kent had hidden depths. And what a transformation it had been when Lorna came out of mourning.

'You're cutting it short, aren't you?' she had felt it necessary to say when Lorna appeared in blue with a hat to match. Her own period of mourning would last the whole year, she and Belle being sisters.

'I heard the cuckoo and thought it was time to make a change.' The cuckoo! What had the cuckoo to do with it? 'Aunt Belle wouldn't have minded.'

There had been only another month to go. All the more reason to wait, one would have thought, but she was young and looked on that day in May quite radiant. She had certainly come into her looks and from then on had taken so much interest in her clothes that Mabel was reminded of her own young days. The Featherstone sisters had always dressed well and Lorna could afford good clothes.

'Now what do you think of this?' she would ask after a shopping trip in Gorsham and she would stand erect against the sitting-room door or stroll about the room to be admired. It seemed a shame that more people didn't see her looking elegant – in a quiet way. Social life in Canterlow was limited in scope. Donnerton was another matter. When in the following spring Dora Liffey invited them for a long weekend, Mabel accepted promptly, taking Lorna's indifferent, 'Yes, if you like' as consent.

The visit was a success. They were made much of by the Liffeys. Cedric met them at the City Station in his new motor car and drove them to High Croft, the Liffeys' comfortable home on the outskirts of the city and with a moorland view. While Mabel hobnobbed with his parents and friends who called to see her, Cedric devoted the weekend to looking after Lorna: on Saturday morning an invigorating walk on Donner Moor; lunch at the

Stormcock Inn: a matinee at the Queen's theatre: an evening at home with the family.

They were joined by Maurice Denby, Rita's fiancé and when they had given up expecting her, Faith Wilbur.

'Forgive me, Mrs Liffey.' She came from the cool darkness outside and stood blinking and smiling in the warm gaslight. 'You must have given me up.'

A pie supper for unemployed ex-servicemen, she explained. She had left early. Before the singsong, she might have added. A time might come when she could hear the wartime songs without heartache, but the smugness of 'Look for the silver lining', now all the rage, was more than she could endure, especially 'rendered' by Ex-Corporal Bilsby's wife. 'I was determined to see Lorna. And how are you, Mrs Hobcroft?'

Out of respect for the pie supper she was wearing grey silk and shoes instead of boots. Not that anyone noticed her clothes except Lorna who felt overdressed and wished she wasn't wearing a gold slave-bangle. Bangles were unnecessary.

Faith was no sooner seated by the fire than they were all roused as never before to the realization that something must be done about unemployed ex-servicemen.

'They had twenty-nine shillings a week for twenty-six weeks after they were discharged: then a pound a week for thirteen weeks. Now they have the ordinary fifteen shillings unemployment benefit.' She came dramatically to a halt, then added slowly and distinctly, 'And that is what they've got for fighting for their country.'

The conversational temperature rose. It was impossible to sit comfortably on one's chair while Faith sat upright on the edge of hers, her eyes blazing.

'It does upset me,' Mrs Liffey confessed, 'when I hear one of those little bands playing in the street and men saying "Thank you" when people drop pennies in a hat. They shouldn't be thanking us after all they did for us.'

'It isn't what they expected,' Cedric said. 'They didn't expect to have to go busking for coppers when they came home.'

'We've been the lucky ones, Ced.' Maurice Denby too had survived, thanks, as he put it, to a piece of shrapnel in his leg, and had returned to a family business.

The arrival of refreshments brought a change of key. Faith joined Lorna on the settee.

'Tell me, how are you? How has it been? You look –' she hesitated: 'beautiful' would embarrass her but she was different in some subtle way, like a flower poised in the one perfect moment when there is no thought of fading '– like a creature from another world.'

'It's wonderful to see you, Faith.' Lorna felt again the warmth and wisdom she had missed without realizing it. There was so much to tell: so much that could not be told. 'I wish—'

They were interrupted by the maid bringing coffee. Faith, having supped on meat pie, declined a cheese puff. The opportunity for real communication escaped them.

'What do you do with yourself?'

Conscious of the range of Faith's own activities, Lorna was at a loss. What on earth did she do with herself? Aunt Mabel overheard and hoisting the family flag, steamed if not into battle, into a strongly defensive position.

'Lorna had a spell of helping the schoolgirls with their needlework,' she said impressively. 'Mr Ushart was very grateful for her help.'

'Mr Ushart?'

'The headmaster,' Lorna breathed, eyes lowered.

'That was a good idea. Girls must know how to sew.' Faith could never be ungenerous even with praise for so modest a contribution to human progress, but Lorna shrivelled and faded into the background with the other ladies while Faith and Mr Liffey, Cedric and Maurice discussed politics and economics – 17.1 per cent of the labour force unemployed; the rapid rise in the cost of living; proposed cuts in government expenditure of £190 million – drifting to lighter topics as the evening wore on.

'A creature from another world.' Was that what she had become? Lorna spent more time than usual in brushing her hair before going to bed. Though healthily tired after a full day, she was some time in falling asleep.

The next morning Cedric drove her to Hookgate to see Aggie, and left her for an hour. It was a poor quarter of the city, low-lying and thickly populated: a network of humble streets, most of the houses of darkened brick, their front steps whitened with donkey-stone in defiance of the soot-pall which rarely rose higher than the chimney pots.

Lorna knew Hookgate well. It was here that she had looked after pale-faced babies and toddlers when their mothers, clogged and shawled, hurried off to work. Aggie was keeping house for her brother Joseph, a joiner by trade, whose wife had died four years ago. They were comfortable together; the little house on the outer fringe of Hookgate was clean and snug.

When Lorna called, Aggie was alone. Joseph had gone to his allotment. He was a dedicated grower of leeks. 'Not that he'd do anything on a Sunday,' Aggie assured her. 'He just likes to keep an eye on them.'

It was an affectionate reunion. To Lorna, Aggie was closer than a relation. They talked more of the times they had shared than of the year that had kept them apart.

'So you're settled in the country,' Aggie said when reminiscences were temporarily exhausted. It was almost an accusation. 'She must be glad to have you with her.' Mrs Hobcroft's high-handed manner at the funeral had not been forgotten.

'Aunt Mabel has been very kind.'

'You'll have a home of your own one of these days. I'm surprised there's not a young man by this time. Oh, all right, I shouldn't have asked – only don't be like your Aunt Belle and let the right one slip through your fingers.'

'Aunt Belle? I didn't know. She never told me.'

'Well, there were reasons why she wouldn't, or shouldn't. It was best kept quiet about.'

'But why? Why should it?'

'Because while she couldn't make up her mind – although I dare say he asked her often enough – to cut a long story short, he went and married somebody else.' Aggie's lips thinned, in disapproval or pain, or the two combined. ' "It's my own fault, Aggie", she said, bless her. And so it is, I told her. You've wakened up too late and missed the boat. There's no putting things right now.'

'That was cruel, Aggie.'

'Yes. I wish now I'd never said those words, true though they were. My heart ached for her even as I said them: she was so upset.'

'I do wish I'd known about it.'

'What would have been the good of that, either to you or her?'

Lorna was saddened. They had shared a great deal but the sharing was incomplete. She had sensed that Belle's lightness was of manner, rather than the outward sign of a shallow nature as her sister had sometimes implied.

'Aunt Mabel must have known. She ought to have known.'

'It all happened years ago and your Aunt Mabel was married and away by that time. She's not the one a broken-hearted girl would have turned to, you must admit. And it was all over long before you were old enough to hear of súch things. But I'm telling a lie. The feeling between them was the kind of thing that's never got over, not by either him or her, seeing each other every day as they did.'

'Every day? Who on earth. . . ? You don't mean. . . ?'

'Morton Liffey, that's who. It can't do any harm to tell you now. You've got sense enough to keep it to yourself and in a way it eases my mind to talk about it. It brings her back from wherever she's gone; and I have many a lonely hour here, dwelling on old times.'

'I did sometimes wonder if Mr Liffey's younger brother. . . .'

That would have been more romantic: a tale of lovers parted by death. But Mr Liffey himself! Not the tragic hero of a drama enacted long ago in the days of wide-brimmed hats trimmed with roses and lily-of-the-valley, and dolmans with gilt buttons – but the father of Cedric and Rita, now prosperous and though not yet portly, a little on the heavy side.

'No, no. Not Albert. It was Morton and Belle that were childhood sweethearts. Perhaps that was why she took him for granted and didn't see the need to settle down until it was too late. New people had come to Offcross Grange, people called Stowe. They were unsettled sort of folk, easy come, easy go, here today and gone tomorrow and with extravagant ways. Miss Belle was dazzled, you might say, and got very friendly with Miss Evelyn Stowe. There was a brother, Rodney. It was common talk that he was taken with Miss Belle. Oh, there's no doubt her head was turned.'

'And then. . . ?'

'The Stowes stayed about two years and it did look as if she had forgotten her other friends. Then they upped all of a sudden and emigrated to Canada. Miss Evelyn wrote a few times and then no more letters came. By the time Miss Belle came to her senses, Morton Liffey was in the clutches of someone else. You couldn't blame him.'

It was obvious now. Aunt Belle's attitude to Mrs Liffey was always polite and pleasant, the pleasant politeness now seen to have been slightly overdone. The informality and ease of other friendships had been missing. Sometimes when aunt and niece had come home after an evening at the Liffeys, Belle had allowed herself a spell of relaxation – a mood equivalent to getting into a dressing gown and slippers.

'Poor Dora will insist on making a show. "It doesn't do to try too hard," she would say. Or "Did you find the pastry heavy?" Or, most damning of all, "Dora does try." '

It was not quite fair but having taken so much, Dora must in justice take a little spiteful criticism as well.'

'I'm sure he would have been much happier with Aunt Belle.' Lorna spoke warmly and without a shred of evidence to support the assertion.

'No doubt of it, as nobody knows better than him,' Aggie said with equal confidence. 'He only had to see the two of them together. That's not to say she hasn't been a good wife to him.'

It had to be admitted that Mrs Liffey was indeed a good, conscientious wife and mother, if somewhat narrow both in views and in person: she was thin – but neat-featured and at her best, handsome.

As they chatted in the little front room, sounds could be heard coming from the kitchen.

'It's Ruth, come to do the potatoes. She lives next door.' Aggie lowered her voice though Ruth couldn't possibly have heard. 'She's badly off with a boy of eight to feed. Just the two of them. I let her help with such things as the potatoes and then she doesn't feel so bad about taking two plates of dinner.'

'She's a widow?'

'He died of wounds in one of them field hospitals. I'll fetch her in. As a matter of fact she hasn't said so but I know she's dying to meet you.'

'Me? Whatever for?'

'She'll tell you.' Aggie went to the door. 'Come along in, Ruth. You can be talking to Miss Lorna while I put the kettle on.'

She was a slim little woman wearing a holland apron over her Sunday skirt and high-necked blouse, with her hair done up in neat braids round her head. She came into the room with a curious air of caution: not furtively or shyly but as if she expected to face some ordeal and was resigned to it.

'My neighbour, Mrs Kirk. And this is Miss Kent that I've helped to look after since she was a baby and I knew her mother before her. Sit down and I'll make us a cup of tea.'

Mystified as to why Mrs Kirk should be dying to see her, Lorna scarcely knew where to begin.

'Aggie tells me you have a little boy, Mrs Kirk.'

'Johnny. And not so little now. He's growing fast. He'll be tall like his father that he's named after.'

'He must be a great comfort to you.'

'He's a good boy, Miss Kent, taking after both sides of the family. Nobody could say a word against anyone on my side and the Kirks – they were good people. All of them.'

She spoke so earnestly and with such emphasis on the last three words that Lorna's interest was roused. Her purpose in coming was plainly not to make conversation: she had come with some message to impart.

'I'm sure he'll do well.'

'No one can be sure how things will turn out.' She was not being wilfully contradictory but stating a universal truth with the authority of experience.

'No, indeed. I believe you have had great sadness in your life.'

Her sympathy brought a softening of the woman's tense expression.

'It's in the past now. I tell myself it's all over and done with. Johnny has been happier since we came here.'

'Then you haven't always lived in Donnerton?'

'We came here three years ago. It was hard at first after being in the country. Then Aggie came and she's been like a sister to me.'

'With me it was the other way round. I moved from town to country. Where do you come from?'

'Canterlow.'

Lorna was now really interested. A small coincidence is usually greeted with a pleasurable sense of the mystery of life, a harmless freak of fate. This was no coincidence. Mrs Kirk's intention was now clear. They were together because she had something to say or something to hear about Canterlow, that other world of

87

which, according to Faith, she herself was now a creature. Simply to hear the name so unexpectedly was to feel the place closing round her as from the beginning it had drawn her in and changed her.

'You lived there?' It was an entirely unnecessary remark, a sort of marking time. Mrs Kirk, having shot her bolt, proceeded with less restraint than before.

'There's a cottage set back a little from the Gorsham road and close to the railway. You can see it from the train. Johnny used to wave at every train that went by and people used to look out for him.'

'I know the cottage. There's a swing hanging from one of the trees. I've often thought it a pity that no one lives there.'

'It's still empty then? Well, it would be too far away from other houses for most folk and it's a lonely road.'

The same could not be said of her present home, hemmed in as it was by tightly packed rows with only narrow cobbled ways between them. The change had been extreme.

'I wanted to ask you, Miss Kent,' – they had evidently come to the crux of their meeting – 'Have you ever heard the name Kirk spoken in Canterlow?'

'Well, no. I haven't. But of course I'm a comparative newcomer. . . .'

'I didn't think you would. It will all have been covered up as if it never happened. If you ask, no one will know anything about it. No one will say a word. They'll stick together. They're like that.' She hesitated. 'I've no right to ask you to do me a favour. . . .'

'What would you like me to do?'

A sudden passion flushed the woman's face and flashed to her eyes. She leaned forward, her palms together, fingers interlocked in an attitude of prayer.

'If ever you hear the name mentioned, tell them the truth – that Ezra Kirk was a good man like his brother and as true to his brother as a man could be. Tell them. Please.' In her urgency her knuckles whitened and were released. She got up.

'I will. I promise. Must you go?'

She nodded. Simultaneously came Cedric's knock on the back door. Her mission accomplished, she went back to the kitchen and soon after, having disposed neatly of the potato peelings, left the house.

The Sunday evening service at the Luke Street chapel was conducted by the Revd Samuel Drake, from whom a rousing sermon could be expected.

'Lorna can't abide lay preachers,' Mabel whispered to Dora Liffey as he went up to the pulpit. 'Oh yes, she has a mind of her own, has Lorna, though you might not think it.'

'And so has Cedric.' His mother's implication was not lost on Mabel. They exchanged smiles and settled themselves in their pew.

'I don't know when I enjoyed a weekend more,' Mabel said as they took off their things at The Birches the next evening.

It was unlike her aunt to strike so hedonistic a note but Lorna too had enjoyed the visit. The air on Donner Moor, as Cedric had reminded her, did more good than all the doctors in the city put together. The upland breeze had freshened her cheeks, bringing a physical exhilaration she had not felt in the deep woods and sheltered lanes of Canterlow for all their allure. She had forgotten the breathtaking views, the sombre panorama of the distant Pennines, the sensation of freedom – and how a solitary rock viewed from a new angle could develop a shoulder, a huge forehead and become a crouching monster sitting out the centuries in a sea of heather.

There had also been reminders of human needs on so vast a scale that by comparison Canterlow itself shrank to the dimensions of a pinpoint. Five minutes with Faith had been enough to make her feel that she had heartlessly abandoned the babies of Hookgate though Faith had not uttered a word of reproach.

'There wasn't much choice,' she had told Cedric amid the

trunks and portmanteaux on the day she left over a year ago; but there was always a choice. Faith had made hers regardless of her own comfort and personal inclinations. Nevertheless for the time being, circumstances (she avoided the tempting word 'fate') kept her here at Canterlow where the quiet river, sheltering trees and rich meadows enhanced the mood in which she was content to exist. If it was wrong to long for what she could never have, surely there could be no harm in praying that everything else would remain unchanged.

# Chapter 10

Lorna had been at Canterlow for almost two years when a letter from her father brought her back to earth with a jolt and alarmed her aunt. How like the man to want to see his daughter all of a sudden after all this time! A long holiday in West Virginia! Money for the voyage! Mabel saw these inducements as the thin end of a wedge designed to separate her from her niece. She could read him like a book. The two children of his second marriage were boys. They must be almost grown up and would very likely leave home. Now that he and his wife were getting older (as we all do – the message was propelled across the Atlantic with silent force) an unmarried daughter could be very useful.

Not that Lorna had shown the least sign of accepting the invitation. The mere thought of leaving Canterlow reduced her to panic. Lying awake, she would marvel that circumstances had combined to bring her there when she might have lived her whole life without ever having seen Adam Ushart, much less known him in the very special way so well suited, she dared to think, to them both. All the same her father had written kindly. Some day perhaps she might go to him and make a short stay, but not yet. Certainly not yet.

Meanwhile she was finding Aunt Mabel's constant harping on

the letter rather tiresome. 'It's not my business to interfere but
. . . you know your own mind . . . I suppose you realize . . . not
easy to feel at home with a stepmother you haven't met. . . .
Strange that after all these years we know so little about her . . .
Belle and I used to wonder but we kept it to ourselves . . .' and
finally 'You're not going out on a day like this.'

'I think I'll pop into Gorsham to see Nora. She'll be coming
home soon and these last days drag for her. Is there anything you
want?'

The day was damp though not cold for the time of year. Thick
mist rising from the Beam shrouded the streets. She was the only
passenger on the platform and at the ticket office.

'Sorry, Miss Kent. There'll be no train to Gorsham this morning. There's thick fog at Donnerton. We'll try to do better for you
tomorrow.'

Feeling reluctant to spend the morning indoors, she turned
up her coat collar, pulled her hat over her ears and set off for a
short walk. There was no suburban fringe to the little town to
delay the transition from streets to open country. The Gorsham
road was deserted. Trees on either side were blurred in outline.
There was no sky. It didn't matter. She was lost in thought, fram-
ing a letter to her father, glad that Nora had not been expecting
her and would not be disappointed, planning what books she
would take next time. She had passed the first milestone when
the stone walls of a cottage appeared on her left, set back from
the road in a neglected garden. There were no trains that day for
small boys to wave to; no small boys to wave. A swing dangled
forlorn from a plum tree, motionless in the windless air. She
turned back, head bowed to avoid the drip of moisture from
overhanging boughs.

'. . . Did you know the Kirks?' she had asked her aunt. 'They
used to live on the Gorsham road.'

'Dear me, I haven't thought of the Kirks for years.' Aunt Mabel
ceased winding wool. Lorna, who was holding the skein, eased

her shoulders. 'I wonder what happened to Mrs Kirk and her boy. The husband died in the war, of wounds.'

'She lives next door to Aggie.'

'Good gracious. Well, it's a small world. I didn't know the woman personally.'

'She mentioned her brother-in-law, Ezra.'

'You surprise me. I should have thought she would keep quiet about him. But being the sort of woman she is. . . .'

'What sort of woman is she?' Lorna asked bluntly, instantly aligning herself with Mrs Kirk whatever the answer might be.

'That's not for me to say.' Aunt Mabel resumed her winding.

'Of course not. You didn't know her personally.'

'There was talk, not without cause, I believe, the husband being overseas, but it was put an end to when the man was found dead. It seems he lost his way in a snowstorm and fell over Canter Edge. The snow lay for a long time and he wasn't found until the thaw came.'

'How sad for her to lose them both. The two brothers.'

'Very sad,' Aunt Mabel said with a look of aversion. 'It doesn't do to speak ill of the dead but as ye sow, so shall ye reap.'

Thinking of little Mrs Kirk peeling potatoes in Hookgate and being grateful presumably for two plates of dinner, Lorna asked no more questions, but mindful of her promise said firmly, 'I liked Mrs Kirk and I believed her when she said that both the Kirks were good men. It seems hard that she should have suffered from malicious gossip as well as from grief.'

Aunt Mabel smiled tolerantly and went on winding. Once Lorna got an idea into her head, one might as well give up. This was another case of lay preachers all over again. . . .


The fog had put Adam Ushart in a quandary. According to regulations, the list of headmasters seeking promotion must be reviewed every year. Applicants were required to present them-

selves for interview at the County Hall in Gorsham. His appointment was for 9.30 a.m. and the railway timetable had been
cancelled for the whole day. Fortunately a word with Alf
Archibald, landlord at the Duke's Arms, was all that was needed
to secure the use of a gig.

'I'll have it ready for you in ten minutes, Mr Ushart.'

It was a pleasure to do him a favour even though he was not a
customer: a real gentleman doing a power of good in the place.

He made an early start: the interview was brief, a mere formality. Nine years ago he had accepted the headship at Canterlow,
confident that he would not stay long in an out-of-the-way overgrown village though he had been lucky to gain promotion so
soon. An early injury in his school days had exempted him from
military service. However the promising launch had left him
becalmed, waiting for a favourable wind. Progress depended on
others: on the death or retirement of some other headmaster.

The school he coveted was at Maywick, within the county
boundary but no more than a mile from Donnerton. It was twice
the size of his school at Canterlow, the salary almost double his
present income. The schoolhouse was late Victorian with
spacious rooms and a proper bathroom, not a room sketchily
fitted with a bath and an unreliable geyser. They could live there
in a manner better suited to Madeline's taste and background.

But Maywick's chief attraction was its proximity to the city
with its lectures, libraries, concerts, theatre, a Literary and
Philosophical Society and many others: also a stimulating mix of
people. He could be content and successful there for the rest of
his career and take an active part in local affairs. The present
head, Birkett, was fifty-seven and unlikely to stay on beyond the
age of sixty. Three more years! A word in the right place helped
in such cases and for that he could count on Councillor Garson.

Meanwhile, a prisoner impatient for release, he had ample
time to brood on his personal problems.

He enjoyed the drive home and wished he had stretched his

resources to set up a horse and gig of his own years ago. Driving gave him the illusion of being in charge, choosing his direction and reaching it in a calculable time, instead of kicking his heels in a place he had quickly outgrown. The steady hoof-beats of the landlord's horse were the only sounds to be heard on the mist-bound road.

Lorna heard them too, behind her and coming nearer, then the light rattle of a gig.

'Miss Kent!'

'Mr Ushart! I didn't expect. . . .'

She looked up at him, her eyes star-lit, her gasp of delight quickly suppressed. How lovely she was, how young and vulnerable! Her devotion so prudently and ineffectually concealed, at first rather amusing like the respectful attentiveness of an anxious pupil, had become important to him. It soothed his pride, assailed from other directions; it was innocently beguiling; it had never threatened his composure or self-command. But now. . . .

'Where are you going on a day like this?'

'Nowhere in particular.' It was true. She had lost all sense of both purpose and direction. Where else in the world could she go when he was there looking down at her? 'Home,' she said, recovering her senses.

'Let me drive you there.' His momentary hesitation had been involuntary, but how could he have driven past with no more than a word, leaving her to follow alone: a friend of his wife, he remembered, as if conscious of questioning eyebrows raised. He leaned over, took her hand and helped her up. His touch thrilled her.

A slight headache, she explained, and the need to think of a reply to a letter from her father. She could think more clearly out of doors. 'I don't want to seem ungrateful if he really wants me to go.'

'Can there be any doubt that he does?'

'He cannot want me in a very personal way. How could he when he doesn't know what sort of person I am? But he may feel it a duty.'

'And you feel that imposes on you an obligation to go.'

'Well, he says,' she took out the letter, ' "You know how poor a letter writer I am. If I don't write it's not because I have forgotten my little girl". Little girl! It's ridiculous.'

'But he obviously is anxious to see you. When will you go?'

'Oh, I'm not going.' She had spoken too quickly. He would wonder why she should stay when she was perfectly free to go. She searched for a safe impersonal reason. 'I don't want to leave Canterlow. It's so beautiful.'

'Even today?'

*Especially today*, she might have said.

'Beautiful, yes.' He had evidently found the reason acceptable. 'But too much enclosed. There have been changes of course but fewer than in most places. Canterlow people have been slow to move, in every sense. Do you know that quite a few of the surnames of the children on our registers are on the manorial rolls in the archives library in Gorsham? Their ancestors were here in the Middle Ages. And in the electoral register there are more and more people with those same names.'

'Do you mean that they're all related?'

'Yes, indirectly. When the population was very small, close relations would marry. . . .' He believed that inherited characteristics, and not only the physical ones could persist from one generation to the next, whether for good or ill. He had sometimes been aware of a collective mood in the place like that of members of a family drawing together in times of crisis.

'But isn't that a good thing?'

'There have been incidents you would not approve of. A place cut off from the outer world may turn in on itself and develop a communal character more powerful than any individual and behaving in ways acceptable neither to the law nor to the

Church. The history of Canterlow might include more than one return to barbarism.'

'But people are more civilized now.' She was not sure what he meant and had only vague ideas of ways unacceptable to the law and the Church: riots perhaps or setting fire to machinery in factories. But there were no factories in Canterlow and his next remark was not reassuring.

'We must hope so – and I must not lecture you.'

She would as always have been content to listen. Sitting so close to him, she positively felt his thoughtful mood and shared it. She also felt the roughness of his sleeve. He wore no gloves. His hands were slim and long-fingered and could be firm, she knew, though he held the reins loosely. His lips too – she saw with so slight a turn of the head that he could not have noticed – were firmly curved but pleasantly upturned as if he might smile. They moved through the mist, alone together as they had never been before. Silence, she discovered, could beget an intimacy unknown when they shared ideas, in however close agreement. For the first time her response to his closeness was ardent: she longed for more than she could ever hope to have; far more than it would be right to take.

Did he too feel the danger of silence? She hoped that he did and was sure that he did not. For whatever reason, he was the first to break it. In other circumstances he might not have felt the necessity. There was certainly no reason to launch at random into an account of his morning and the importance of reaching the County Hall despite the cancellation of the trains.

'Oh, but you're not leaving—'

'No, no. . . . Not yet. It was just routine.' He regretted having broached the subject and especially to her. It implied a lack of immediate personal success, a flaw in the vision of him she had conjured up. Absurdly highly coloured as it was, he had no wish to destroy it.

'I'm sure a great many people would be sorry if you ever did leave Canterlow.' Her voice was gentle and hesitant.

'It's good of you to say so.'

There had been no lapse from formality. Yet for her as they talked of West Virginia, gigs and interviews, it was as if another kind of communication had been narrowly averted. When the gig lurched over an unevenness in the road she was thrown towards him. If she had leaned a little further to the right her head would have rested on his shoulder, his sleeve touching her cheek. How awful if he thought. . . . She sat upright and was sufficiently herself as they came towards the first houses to suggest that he should let her get down.

'I shall enjoy walking home. My headache's almost gone.'

He made no demur. She had always behaved correctly and in this case with perfect delicacy. The arrival of Miss Kent and Mr Ushart together in Archibald's gig would not, even in the thickest mist nature could devise, pass unnoticed and escape comment; whereas if Miss Prior had been his passenger he could have driven her to her lodgings in the Square for all Canterlow to see. The thought came unbidden, its implication clear: startlingly so, especially as it brought with it a new awareness of the girl herself.

'Thank you.' Looking up, she saw a change in him. It was as if he had never seen her before.

She was right. There was nothing alluring in her damp mackintosh, buttoned up and tightly belted, nor in her hat, close-fitting as a nun's coif. Not an inch of her person was visible except a strand of dark hair on her forehead; her face, unlined in its youthful freshness; her eyes, slightly troubled but raised to look at him as if there were nothing else in the world to see. Yet she stirred in him a sudden wave of passionate desire that almost overwhelmed him: a quickened pulse; a dizziness. Her touch of bashfulness was irresistibly appealing as it should be in her awakening; and how easily it could be overcome, how willingly she would submit. Their eyes met. His lips parted. They shaped her name. 'Lorna.' She understood, flushed and turned away.

It was over in a moment. As man and woman they had met at last and could never meet innocently again. For him it had been as poignant as for her but recognized at once as an impulse such as any man might feel when alone with a lovely girl, young and unspoilt and – he must admit – already devoted to him. Mercifully it had passed but its effect had been restorative: it had bolstered his confidence which had sometimes wavered under other pressures. He felt too some pride in his self-control. The danger of losing it had been so short-lived as to make it negligible, though his brow was wet and not only from moisture in the air. He wiped it with the back of his hand as he drove on. His conscience, thank God, was perfectly clear.

For her it was as if a barrier had fallen: they had been no longer separate from each other but suddenly together in mutual desire. He had breathed her name. Miss Kent and Mr Ushart had vanished, leaving Adam and Lorna, both of them, she felt in her confusion, unrecognizable. The thrill of knowing that he could have loved her was followed instantly by the certainty of loss. In thinking of him now there could only be conflict and thinking of him was all that was left to her. They must not be alone together again. In dreaming of him she had been content: dreaming is timeless and inconsequential. The dream had become reality for just long enough to change everything.

Without him Canterlow would be a wilderness. Trudging home, hands in pockets, she fingered her father's letter. It was a sign. She must go to him. He wanted to see her and she was lucky, she reminded herself drearily, in having somewhere to go. Some girls far more bitterly disappointed in love had their hearts broken and had nowhere to go except to. . . .

But there was no comparison between her and Alice Hood. She had expected nothing, wanted nothing and therefore could not be disappointed. Based on a false premise, the argument naturally rang hollow and certainly brought no comfort. In the days that followed, comfort was hard to find. Gradually, in brooding over the incident – feeling again the cool air, the mystery of the way ahead, the smell of sodden grass, the way he had leaned forward, his eyes all at once darker, his lips parted – she made a discovery. A dangerous corner had been avoided. If they had gone that way, he would have become no longer master but lover, to be loved in return but to be less revered. As it was, he had almost stepped down from his pedestal and come more nearly to her own level. Ignorant though she was, she knew that in his arms, if he had been free, she could have been rapturously happy; but now that they were apart she knew that the pedestal had been important and wondered sadly if love, which should be uplifting, in some way brought one down to earth. She had grown older.

With a valiant effort she summoned up her share of the Featherstone common sense and behaved very much as usual, giving no sign of her inward tumult. She wrote to her father five times and each time tore the letter up, posted the sixth, thanking him for his kind invitation and remained unable to make up her mind whether to go or stay. She was still undecided when news came from Hookgate. Dear faithful Aggie was critically ill: it was pneumonia. Knowing that there would be no one to look after her, Lorna went at once to Donnerton.

# Chapter 11

Nurse Thorsby was experienced and competent. She also contrived, while doing all that was required for her patient, to make it clear that she was stretching a point in accepting an engagement in Hookgate. She was used to a different class of patient in better parts of the city.

The houses in Hookgate had not been designed for invalids: a kitchen and front room, a steep and narrow staircase, two small bedrooms and one cold tap had been deemed adequate provisions for a family. It had been enough for two healthy adults and South Terrace had the advantage of a water closet in the back yard, whereas houses on the northern and older side had not been modernized beyond the point of having one earth closet each.

In Aggie's room the double bed left only narrow spaces on either side. Nurse Thorsby was large. Bending over her patient, she came into immediate contact with a wall behind her. Remaking the bed was impossible when there was nowhere to put the patient. Everything but the washstand and wardrobe and one chair had to be removed to Joseph's room.

'You should have got her into hospital, Miss Kent. People like this cannot expect to be professionally nursed at home.'

Detesting her, Lorna knew that she was right but Aggie had

begged so piteously to be kept at home that there was no alternative.

'Let me die,' she had gasped, 'but don't put me in hospital. Let me die in my own bed.'

Fortunately she did not die. Lorna slept in the front room downstairs on a camp bed supplied by the Liffeys, sat with Aggie during Nurse Thorsby's time off, kept the kitchen fire going for hot water, carried coal up to the tiny bedroom fire and carried ashes down, emptied buckets and chamber-pots, and had a meal ready for Joseph when he came home from work. Ruth Kirk did shopping and took her turn in sitting with Aggie at night. She would see to Joseph's meals while Aggie convalesced at The Birches.

When the crisis was passed and Aggie could be left for a while, Lorna and Ruth occasionally spent a companionable hour by the sitting-room fire and grew confidential. Ruth had been born at Canterlow and although resigned to never going back, she naturally suffered pangs of homesickness and took a melancholy pleasure in hearing of people she knew. Miss Prior, for instance, had taught Johnny until he stopped going to school.

'They were saying things that upset him. The other children. It wasn't their fault. They heard what was said at home. That was before his Uncle Ezra died. Then afterwards when I told Mr Ushart we would be leaving, "It's the best thing you could do, Mrs Kirk," he said. "Johnny can begin again elsewhere and so can you".'

By this time Lorna had formed a clearer picture of the ordeal she had endured and knew the kind of thing that was being said about Ruth and her brother-in-law. Ruth herself had first heard of the gossip from Johnny who didn't understand what people had against his uncle – and was involved in several fights.

'It was only at night that Ezra could come. He was single-handed at the farm except for old Tom the cowman. He'd promised John that he would keep an eye on us. I heard them talking on the last night of John's leave. "Don't you worry," Ezra said. "I'll see to Johnny and if Ruth needs anything she just has to say." It was a two-mile walk for him from the farm and two miles back after he'd been working from dawn to dusk but he came regular, twice a week. Needless to say there were those that were quick to say he came for the wrong reasons.'

There was much worse to come. It was a tale to be told in whispers and in no more light than came from the small fireplace in Joseph's front room.

'It started among two or three. One night when Ezra was leaving – it was after midnight – a motor car went past coming from Gorsham. I was standing with the door open as Ezra went to the gate and couldn't see who was in it. But Ezra said that one of them was Councillor Garson. After that the story grew and spread.'

The climax came when two or three local men happened to come home on leave.

'They made a great to-do in the Ploughman's Arms about John being cheated while he was away fighting for his country. The next time Ezra came, I think they must have been waiting for him as he walked off in the dark. That was the last time I ever saw him. He never got home that night.'

'I heard that he was lost in a snowstorm.'

'There was no snow that night. Tom was up early the next morning at the farm. There was no sign of Ezra. The snow came two days later.'

'Would he pass Canter Edge on the way home?'

'He wouldn't go anywhere near the Edge. The lane to the farm keeps well away from it. Anyway, he knew every inch of the way blindfold.'

'What are you telling me, Ruth?'

'I'm telling you of wickedness past belief. God forsook Canterlow that night and the devil himself came into his own. Nobody rightly knows what happened but as sure as I'm sitting here they killed him and threw him over the Edge – or it might have been the other way round.'

Had Adam been thinking of Ezra Kirk when he spoke of a return to barbarism? It had been trial and execution without reference to the law by men who cared nothing for the Church.

'Afterwards' – Ruth's face was white, the room dark as the fire died – 'what hurt me most for Ezra's sake was that nobody talked about it. Nobody said it was a wicked shame. They may have said it among themselves but I never heard a word of sympathy. They tarred me with the same brush as they tarred Ezra with. I was lucky,' she said bitterly, 'not to go over the Edge as well.'

Old Tom had been the only one to share her grief. All that she knew was what he had been able to tell her. Mercifully neither brother knew of the other's death. She had heard that John was missing before Ezra died. Then had come the dreaded telegram. By that time Ezra too was gone.

It was late when Ruth left. Lorna stood on the back step until she heard her slide the bolt of her own door a few feet away. A fierce light from one of the forges suddenly set the sky ablaze then died slowly, leaving only the stars. Hookgate was never absolutely at rest. A baby cried; a gate was closed; a pair of clogged feet passed close by and could be heard growing fainter on the cobbles for almost a minute. There was nothing to fear – not here.

She remembered how sometimes in the Beam Valley when trees were heavy with foliage and water shimmered in veiled sunlight, she had seemed to feel more in the air than was revealed: a sense of waiting; a suspense often rapturous but not always so; an atmosphere brooding and mysterious. In Canterlow a girl's body could be recovered from the dam without anyone knowing how it came to be there – or for how long. A man's body could be found in melting snow and the same silence enveloped it. It occurred to her that if Alice Hood's seducer should ever be identified, he might be as savagely dealt with as Ezra Kirk had been and with more justification.

All the same she was glad to go back, taking Aggie with her for a long convalescence. It was spring before she wrote to her father again, explaining that she was not free to leave at present. By that time she had found another excuse for staying.

# Chapter 12

It was on a Friday afternoon in April that Lorna became involved in a new dilemma of a different kind. She happened to be trespassing in the school building. No one knew that she was there except the caretaker who was sworn to secrecy.

'You'll be all right, Miss Kent. Take your time. You've got the place to yourself. Mr Ushart comes in again at six on Fridays to check the registers – and then I lock up.'

'I shall be gone long before that, Mr Coxon.'

Nothing but the urgent need to finish Aggie's nightdresses would have induced her to sneak into the end classroom like this. Despite Coxon's assurance that she was perfectly safe, she felt very much on edge. There would have been no objection to her using the treadle machine: it would have been taken for granted. It was dread of meeting Adam there that stiffened her fingers as she threaded and made her drop the scissors and scatter pins, ears cocked in case he came back earlier than expected as he had done once before.

The long seams were quickly done. Noiselessly, as if the walls had ears, she replaced the cover, folded the nightdresses and went to the door. She was closing it behind her when to her astonishment she saw at the other end of the hall another person behaving in exactly the same way. A boy on tiptoe in his socks, his boots tied round his neck by their laces, was emerging with even greater caution than hers from the classroom at the other end. He saw her a second or two before she saw him and stood stock still as if paralysed. They gazed at each other, frozen in mutual silence.

The need to preserve it was obscure but infectious. Lorna was wearing her shoes but she contrived to reach him without a sound. He was ten or eleven years old. She recognized him as Lennie Trimdon, one of Captain Hook's pirates, looking both guilty and woebegone.

'What *have* you been doing, Lennie?'

'Please miss, I haven't been doing anything.'

'But why are you still here? Everybody else has gone home.' She glanced at her watch. 'An hour ago.'

It was too much. Lennie's spirit failed him. Tears spilled over his cheeks and fell on his jersey.

'Mr Moxby kept me in, miss, because I didn't know anything about India. It wasn't my fault. When they did about India I was absent with boils. And I won't half get wrong for being late when the tea's ready and when my Dad comes home he'll skin me alive for not seeing to the hens. . . .'

The upper half of the classroom door was glazed; she could see Mr Moxby in his high chair: that is, she could see enough of a masculine figure to assume that he was there. It was iniquitous to keep a child in for so long and for such a reason. For Lennie the hour must have been an eternity. But the bootless feet, the furtive opening of the door. . . ?

'Did you explain to Mr Moxby that you had to see to the hens?'

'No, miss. I. . . .'

'But he did say you could go home?'

'No, miss. He. . . .'

'He didn't?'

'No, miss. I think Mr Moxby's dead, miss.'

Horror-stricken and trembling, yet with quiet reverence, Lorna approached the seated figure at the desk. He had fallen forward and lay with his tangled dark hair on his hands – and his hands on an expanse of white paper. His face was turned away. She saw the back of his neck – a portion of his throat – and went furiously back to the door.

'It's all right, Lennie, Mr Moxby isn't dead.' She spoke more loudly than usual – they had been whispering – and added for decency's sake, 'He just isn't very well.' The relief in the child's face made her angrier still. 'And if you're a good boy and behave yourself, Mr Moxby will never keep you in again. Put your boots on and tell your mother I said it wasn't your fault.'

She was more than ready to say it again as she shook Mr Moxby awake. He raised his head, heavy-eyed, and propped it on a listless arm, moistened his dry lips and saw her without recognition.

'Mr Moxby, you should be ashamed of yourself.'

The brisk tone penetrated his stupefaction.

'Miss Kent!'

'You heard what I said.'

He nodded. 'I'm always ashamed of myself. I have nothing whatever to be proud of.'

'Do you realize that you kept Lennie Trimdon here for a whole hour? He was beside himself.'

'Good Lord! The poor little beggar. Where is he?'

'Gone home to be thrashed for being late.' But Lorna spoke less sharply. Between Lennie's wretchedness and Moxby's there was little to choose. 'He thought you were dead.'

'I wish I was. Believe me, every day of my life I wish I was dead.'

She did believe him. He was feeling for a handkerchief in a bulging pocket, then in another, found it in a third and wiped his face. Realizing that she was still standing, he half rose and in doing so caught sight of the paper on which his greasy head had rested.

'My God! – Just look at that. What time is it?'

She recognized it as an open page of the Board of Education Attendance Register, a sacred ledger. She had seen Miss Prior's with its immaculate pattern of neat black lines all sloping at the same angle, occasional O's for absence and totals in red. The one on the desk had a slovenly, devil-may-care look about it.

'I was trying to balance the damned thing.'

'Let me see.'

'It's easy really. The figures in the end column have to add up to the same number as the every day totals at the bottom. I'm thick-headed at any time but by the end of the week. . . .'

It was perfectly clear that his thick-headedness was thickened still further by misspent evenings and sleepless nights; yet she was strangely reluctant to leave him to muddle on for who knew how long, especially when he said, 'Got to get it right before he comes back. Ushart.'

Her dread of his finding her there was probably more acute than Moxby's but having grasped what was needed, she began to enter the figures. It was only a matter of careful checking and simple addition. In ten palpitating minutes it was done.

'What can I say?' He was pathetically grateful. 'He checks them on Fridays and locks them away where neither moth nor rust doth corrupt and where thieves do not break through nor steal. He can be pretty scathing, you know, but to be fair, I give him plenty to be scathing about.'

'You're not happy in your work, are you?'

'Happy?' His eyes clouded. 'I've forgotten what it's like.'

They went into the hall. He put the register on top of the others on the headmaster's desk.

'Why don't you stick your head under the cold tap?' It was the equivalent of telling Lennie to dry his eyes.

'I'll do that.' He went into the cloakroom. She waited until the splashing ceased and from the window saw him crossing the yard in his shirt sleeves, his jacket under one arm as he mopped his face with his handkerchief.

'Why don't you take him on?' Nora had a soft spot for Roy Moxby. 'And lick him into shape.'

People didn't do things like that but Nora had rightly judged that the man needed help. One couldn't help pitying a miserable fellow creature when one knew from experience what it was like to be unhappy, though the even tenure of 'her own life had never been disturbed as for some reason Moxby's had been – and Hamlet's. He too had an unsympathetic stepfather as well as other problems, including Ophelia. Was Moxby suffering from an unsuccessful love affair?

The strain of comparing Moxby with the unfortunate prince occupied her as she went up Abbot's Lane – and trod on a wallet. She scarcely needed to look inside, where a dog-eared visiting-card declared the owner's identity. She remembered the jacket under his arm, the bulging pockets. . . .

'I found Mr Moxby's wallet in Abbot's Lane,' she told her aunt.

'You'd better send Gladys round with it. He'll be in a rare state without it.'

'He may not know that he's lost it. He's careless about his things. Actually I'd rather like to take it myself. I might meet the Mighty Councillor.'

'You're more likely to meet Mrs Garson. He's never at home. She's a nice enough little body but she hasn't much life left in her.'

'Crushed' was Aunt Mabel's word and it was apt, Lorna felt, when later in the evening she called at the Garsons' home, one of half a dozen bay-windowed houses in Alexandra Street. Mrs Garson herself opened the door. She was a thin woman with the sagging appearance of having once been buxom, with dark hair and eyes and a vague, apologetic manner.

'Just like him.' She took the wallet. 'I'm sorry you had the bother. He's gone out again and didn't mention losing it. I've seen you about, Miss Kent. Mrs Hobcroft and I used to see more of each other in times gone by but I don't get out much now.'

As they exchanged a few words on the doorstep, Lorna felt herself being surreptitiously looked at and presently—

'I don't have much company. Will you not come in for a few minutes? I knew your aunt, Miss Featherstone, when she used to come to her sister's, from the time you were a little girl.'

In the front sitting-room they sat at the window, between them a small table and a large aspidistra. Curtains and carpet were in various shades of brown. Pictures framed in dark oak hung on a buff wallpaper.

'I like to see people going past, you know.' They could be seen in segments between the broad shining leaves of the aspidistra. She fingered the wallet as she talked, turning it over and over. Suddenly she put it down on the table and burst out, 'What am I to do with him, Miss Kent? It's breaking my heart to see the way he is and never a smile on his face. I shouldn't talk to you like this. He's nothing to you. You've never known him as he really is.'

Lorna's gaze followed hers to a photograph on the upright piano.

'Yes. That's Roy. It was taken just before he went to the College.'

The face was clear-cut; the faint smile and the posture of the head expressed youthful confidence.

'He was pleased to go?'

'Pleased to go and pleased to get away from here. That's the truth of it.'

There was plainly more to come. Lorna got up and looked more closely at the photograph.

'I believe he's a sensitive person, Mrs Garson, and courteous.'

'There now. You understand. Miss Featherstone was like that. What a pity she was taken so soon.'

Lorna's heart warmed to her: no one else had spoken to her

of Aunt Belle in that way.

As a small boy, it seemed, Roy had been full of promise. He took after his father, who owned a small bookshop in Donnerton. 'A true gentleman,' Mrs Garson said with feeling. 'Only he passed away when Roy was seven years old.' She had come to live in Canterlow where she had relatives. 'He could read when he was four, and such a memory. I wish you could have heard him recite. He wasn't shy in those days.'

'I wonder – could it have been Roy, the little boy who recited the whole of *The Wreck of the Hesperus*, word perfect, at a concert?'

'You knew about that?'

'I was there!'

His mother beamed. Nothing could have delighted her more. They parted friends.

'You'll come again?'

'I'd like to.'

'There was something rather depressing about Mrs Garson,' she remarked at supper.

'The something depressing about Mrs Garson is Councillor Garson,' was her aunt's crisp reply.

'She didn't mention her husband. It's Roy she's worried about.'

'And no wonder. It was the biggest mistake she ever made to marry that bombastic thick-skinned cock-of-the-walk. She and Roy would have been far better on their own.'

Lorna had heard Councillor Garson speak on behalf of Baldwin in advance of the election to be held next month. Her aunt had described him perfectly, omitting only his truculent moustache. Her own first impression had been of his size: he was over six feet in height, broadly built, with a massive head, red complexion and a shock of thick waving hair. To a nervous small boy he must have seemed a giant, or an ogre, bending over his bed, for instance, or towering a few feet away in a small room. Moreover, she recalled with growing distaste, it could have been Councillor Garson who started the scandalous rumours leading to Ezra Kirk's death.

'She's lonely,' she said reverting to Mrs Garson. 'Couldn't we ask her to tea or something? You'd do her a world of good.'

Mabel softened, could be said to purr. For a young person Lorna was surprisingly sound in judgement.

Lorna was learning among other things how useful a father in West Virginia could be as a fulcrum for her lever in the management of her aunt. The period of her indecision as to whether to go to him or not had been an uneasy one for Aunt Mabel too.

'You've been happy here, haven't you?' she had asked quite tearfully on one occasion when Lorna appeared for the third or fourth time with a letter ready for the post. 'We've managed very well together.'

'You know I've been happy,' Lorna said and went on smoothly, 'and I'm getting used to my room. One can get used to anything in time.'

'Your room? You couldn't have a pleasanter room. It's more sunny and spacious even than the spare room.'

'It would be a lovely room if. . . . Well, if I could see more of it. I think I should feel more settled in it if there was somewhere to sit besides the bed – more space, I mean,' she added quickly lest another chair should be provided, 'and if I could open the window without squeezing between the wardrobes.' She looked at the clock and the letter in her hand.

Aunt Mabel rose, trod rather heavily up the stairs, Lorna following, flung open the door of the room and stood in its restricted centre.

'There's far too much furniture in here,' she said accusingly. 'I hadn't realized. Why didn't you tell me? It seemed wrong to part with things that would be your own some day and then there were the things that were your own already to be fitted in.

It was for your own good.'

'All that you do is for my own good, Aunt Mabel.' It was Adam who had said that encouragement could be more effective than fault-finding; and Aunt Mabel's assumption that she would have a home of her own some day brought another pang: she would never marry, never have a home entirely her own.

A few days later the news of Aggie's illness had spurred on the reorganization. The heavy Victorian pieces were sent to a furniture repository in Gorsham. A small room next to Gladys's was furnished for the invalid with some of the others. When Lorna returned from her long stay in Donnerton, the transformation was complete.

'I thought we might as well have it papered while we were at it.' Aunt Mabel looked round the half-denuded room with approval. It was indeed as sunny and spacious as she had claimed.

'I wouldn't have believed it.' Lorna was rather ashamed of her indirect approach but it had drawn them together. As well as a triumphant sense of achievement, Aunt Mabel had the added pleasure of telling her friends that she had been 'modernizing' her niece's room.

On the first of May there would be the crowning of Canterlow's May Queen, a maypole, a procession and tea for the schoolchildren. Lorna suggested that the teachers might be invited to round off the evening at The Birches: Miss Prior, Miss Ellwood, Mr Moxby and the new man Mr Shackleton, a middle-aged bachelor interested in stamp-collecting.

'And Mrs Garson too,' she added. 'She would like to see Roy enjoying himself for a change.'

It seemed unlikely, but in a cheerful atmosphere among people he knew, he did appear if not joyful at least less miserable. The others had never seen him looking so smart – in a dark suit, starched white collar and well-pressed trousers, with a white handkerchief folded to a triangle in his breast pocket.

'Hasn't his mother turned him out nice,' Miss Ellwood whispered, and while Mr Shackleton bored the ladies with information about stamps, Roy helped Gladys with trays, handed refreshments out and made himself agreeable. At the end of a game of whist he demonstrated a card trick and bowed to applause; but he refused point blank to recite *The Wreck of the Hesperus*.

'I had my moment of fame,' he said.

'You've forgotten the words,' Miss Ellwood said.

'Forgotten?' His mother looked at him fondly. 'Roy never forgets anything.'

Glances were exchanged and smiles suppressed. What about the globe, the pen nibs, the entries in the register? What about Lennie Trimdon?

But when they gathered round the piano with the door left open so that Aggie could hear, it was Roy who knew all the verses of 'Keep the home fires burning', 'K-K-K-Katie' and 'Roses are blooming in Picardy'.

'Wish I had your memory,' Mr Shackleton said, and went on to tell how forgetting the time of a train had caused him to miss an opportunity of buying an early Gold Coast stamp. What a bore the man was!

But it was not boredom that had suddenly clouded Roy's face. Lorna noticed the change at once. A sudden glumness had descended and lasted for the rest of the evening.

'Mrs Garson and I had a good talk,' Aunt Mabel said when the guests had left and they were putting the room straight. 'You were right. She is worried about Roy. He seemed a nice enough young fellow to me.' She yawned. It had been a pleasant evening to be talked over in detail, but not now.

In her spacious newly papered bedroom, Lorna considered the case of Roy Moxby. What had caused his sudden change of mood? He had seemed – what was the word – worried? Harassed? 'I wish I had your memory,' Mr Shackleton had said and gone on about his silly stamp. Some things were best forgotten but one could be haunted by a memory. That was the word. Haunted.

# Chapter 13

Lorna kept her promise and called on Mrs Garson from time to time. She was always made welcome and urged to come again.

'We're never short of things to talk about,' Mrs Garson said on one such visit and went on talking about Roy. It was like listening to a story with only one character. The compulsion of the narrator to tell it compelled the listener's attention. Her account of her son's character and achievements was naturally one-sided. Of the fecklessness and indifference to his work and their detrimental effect on his pupils she was either ignorant or oblivious. No mention was made of his nights out in Gorsham, his return on the last train or his reluctance to get up in the morning.

'He's clever. Always was. Clever like his father and like him in so many other ways. Thoughtful. Forever reading. Never quite like other boys.' He had never cared for rough games. What he did like, even when he was just a schoolboy, was to go off on his own to fish in the Beam up above the dam. It was just the same when he was a student home for the vacation. 'He'd spend whole days there. A dreamer, Miss Kent. Always was.'

Roy had been nine years old when his mother married again. 'It was him I was thinking of – and his education. His father left nothing. There wasn't much money in books. To tell you the truth Mr Garson needed a housekeeper. I'd have been well content just to come and keep house for him but he said people

119

would talk and in his position he couldn't do with talk. So it was marriage or nothing. Of course a housekeeper is what I am, most of the time.'

The thought of the other times silenced her. Lorna looked tactfully out of the window, speculating on the possible drawbacks in being married to Councillor Garson, and saw between the leaves of the aspidistra a baker's tray moving up the street apparently without support.

'He should have gone to the University but Mr Garson didn't see his way to supporting him for another year. Two years at the College was as much as he was prepared to pay for. He'd be earning his living a year sooner and he'd be sure of a teaching post. Mr Garson is on the Education Committee,' his wife confided with innocent pride. She was in many ways a stupid woman. In marriage there can be drawbacks on both sides.

In the course of several visits Lorna learned a good deal about Roy Moxby. Polite attention to his mother's anecdotes developed into genuine interest which in its turn was to become fascination. No prompting was needed. She had learned not to interrupt, not having recovered from the answer to one question she had unwisely put.

'What about Roy's friends, Mrs Garson? There must have been girls, or a girl.'

'There's surely no need for *you* to ask *that*, Miss Kent.' The archness of Mrs Garson's reply had been overpowering.

But apparently there had been one girl. His mother had deduced it from Roy's behaviour: he had not breathed a word of it to her. It could not have amounted to much but he had seemed more cheerful for some reason, and that made it all the worse when he fell into such a low state.

With her quiet voice, her subdued manner and her ruthless adherence to one topic, she established a firm hold on her audience. There were times when Lorna, rigid in her chair, felt trapped like a specimen moth impaled on a pin; or mesmerized and unable to look anywhere except at her hostess's moving lips until, her strained muscles suddenly relaxing, she came to herself with a start, murmured that she must go and escaped.

She was forming the curious impression that there were two Roy Moxbys: the one she saw occasionally and the one whom no one had ever seen, except his mother. So many of her verbs were in the past tense: he was clever, he never liked games, he used to read a lot – that the Roy she spoke of could have died years ago and she, Lorna, was listening to his elegy. The cadences of Mrs Garson's voice were invariably melancholy.

'Always was,' she kept on saying. Never 'Still is.'

Lorna's mental picture of the Roy who always was but was not so now was rather attractive. In appearance he was like the photograph on the piano, not dishevelled in a scruffy suit but casually dressed, canvas bag slung over his shoulder or rod in hand, dreamily angling in a quiet reach of the Beam west of the dam, or prone among moon-daisies, his eyes glued to a book. More than once as the mournful voice droned on she grew drowsy and lost her hold on reality. The stuffy little room became a dark brown pool in which she was being willingly submerged.

When did she feel the first prick of uneasiness? Once – it was a warm day – she must actually have dozed off and came to herself suddenly. Something had wakened her. There had been a change. It was in fact no more than the temporary cessation of Mrs Garson's monologue. Feeling ashamed of her rudeness, Lorna roused herself to speak and said the first thing that came into her head.

'What made him change?'

It was a foolish question. People could change gradually for all sorts of reasons – hating their work or their stepfathers or at the onset of an illness or for a number of small things combined. But Mrs Garson took it seriously enough to pause before answering. When she did speak it was not in the maundering monotone

Lorna had grown used to but in a more sensible, thoughtful and therefore more arresting way.

'I wish I knew. Before God I wish I knew.' Her dark eyes met Lorna's directly. They expressed more than gravity. Was it desperation?

Whatever it was it changed the atmosphere. The uneasiness Lorna had begun to feel sharpened into alarm. She hesitated to ask the obvious questions lest the answers should confirm a foreboding already forming in her mind.

'When did it happen?' she brought herself to ask. 'How long ago?'

'When? It was in the last year of the War. At about this time of the year. On a Sunday.'

In the afternoon Roy had gone off on one of his long walks. Sometimes he went by the riverside path to Fordham, and had tea at the inn.

'We'd had ours before he came back and whether he'd had his I never knew.' They had heard him come in and go straight upstairs. 'I called, "Have you had your tea, Roy?" He didn't answer and Mr Garson said, "Leave him be and stop fussing." But I went up. He was lying on his bed, staring at the ceiling. I said, "Will you be all right or would you like one of those headache powders?" "Of course I'm all right," he said. "You might have taken your boots off, love, before lying on your bed," I said. That's all I said although I could see there was mud on the counterpane already. I felt sure there was something wrong and it started on that very day.'

A Sunday – in August – in the last year of the War. Surely Mrs Garson must have made the connection as she herself had done immediately, between the sudden change in Roy and the death of Alice Hood. Everyone would be talking about it. There had been a girl, his mother said; he never talked about her but for a time he had been cheerful – and then. . . ? Could he have been in love with Alice Hood and so shattered by her death that he was still haunted by the memory of it? Could he possibly have been the man in black? Remembering Mrs Garson's hints about the present state of his affections, she made up her mind to bring her acquaintance with both mother and son to an end.

But the story of Alice Hood had become a fixation. She had never discussed it with her aunt but the need to settle certain details now seemed imperative.

'I was thinking of the Hoods the other day,' she remarked conversationally. 'Wasn't it sad – about Alice, I mean? Especially sad to think of her going to chapel on a lovely summer evening in the usual way and then for that to happen.'

'I don't know where you get your going to chapel and your summer evening from.' Aunt Mabel put down her tapestry and took off her glasses. 'It was a wet morning when she was found and she'd been there a long time. It was never known how long.'

'Can't think where I got hold of the idea that she was found on a Sunday,' Lorna said mendaciously. 'You know how people talk.'

So much for the theory that news of Alice's death had sent Roy Moxby to his room, to stare distraught at the ceiling without removing his boots. There remained a much more worrying possibility. Could he have been reduced to that state, not by the news but by the fact of her death? Had he known before anyone else that Alice was dead? For the first time it occurred to her that she might have been wrong in assuming that Alice had drowned herself in despair immediately after parting from her lover. There could have been an interval in which he came back.

Who was he? Not a stranger to the district but an outsider with no confidential friendships nor any close connections in Canterlow? A man who from boyhood had spent whole days in the vicinity of Miller's Dam and beyond, by the quiet waters of the Beam? Could he also be cruel, not by nature but from fear of losing his job, or of his stepfather, and afterwards be half crazed with remorse?

Roy Moxby certainly lacked courage. He had told her so. They

123

had once met by chance in Fold Lane and had walked home together. Mrs Garson's hints could not have been wider of the mark, but the incident in the end classroom and the May Day festivities had drawn them into a comradeship of sorts. One of the newspapers was running a series of reports on acts of courage in wartime under the title 'Undecorated Heroes'.

'Courage is the quality I most admire,' she had said, wishing she had more of it.

'It's a gift. You have to be born with it. Personally I wasn't. I'll tell you straight, Lorna. I'm a coward.'

'You're not the only one. I've only recently screwed up courage to tell Aunt Mabel that the furniture in my room was driving me mad. Even so I didn't put it like that.'

'Because you thought it might upset her. You don't know what it's like to be a genuine, low-down coward, not so much physically, but with people. I've been afraid of them all my life. I wouldn't have minded joining up with the risk of being blown to bits. It was the other men I couldn't have faced up to.'

'It might have been your salvation,' Lorna said priggishly. With Roy one slipped easily into the role of sage elderly aunt.

'Rheumatic fever was my salvation. At least I thought so at the time but now I'm not so sure. Being blown to bits might have saved me from worse things including the rut I'm in now.'

'I believe I'm in a rut too,' she said with a swift change of role.

'But you don't share your rut with Councillor Garson.'

'He's as weak as water,' Nora had said but she had a soft spot for him and she too would feel less contempt for his weakness than respect for his honesty in confessing it. Lorna was still wondering if the man she had seen could have been Roy when an odd little incident revived her memory of the Sunday evening when she had gone to the Hammond house to inspect the apple crop.

So far she had been lucky. Councillor Garson had never been at home when she called and she was determined not to go again. But as a favour to Aunt Mabel she did deliver an invitation to Mrs Garson to attend a meeting of the District Nursing Association.

Mrs Garson greeted her less heartily than usual. She seemed flustered and apologized for taking her visitor straight into the kitchen where the scrubbed deal table was covered with the scattered contents of a tin box: buttons, buckles, parts of watches, keys, penshafts, broken brooches.

'Mr Garson will be here any minute. I've turned the house upside down and I haven't been able to find what he wants.' She held up a small object between the thumb and forefinger of her left hand and rummaged hopelessly with her right. 'Oh my, there he is now.'

They were at the back of the house but the iron gate was opened and clashed to with such force that they heard it, then felt the floor vibrate as the front door was slammed and heavy feet trod the narrow passage – and he was there in the doorway. At close quarters he was even more impressive, larger in every sense than on a political platform: a man with the whole weight of public affairs in Canterlow on his shoulders and shoulders broad enough to bear it. Lorna was chiefly intimidated by his moustache: dense, brown, inches deep, stiffly bristling, the long ends waxed and pointing downward to his outward thrusting lower jaw.

'It's just Miss Kent.' Mrs Garson's apologetic introduction increased Lorna's sensation of being of no account but his cursory nod annoyed her.

'How do you do, Mr Garson.' She spoke clearly, her articulation of the word Mister particularly distinct and inclined her head slightly. One could not give him a straight look: he was too big. Looking up, one saw into the nostrils flaring above the moustache. She chose to look away. He ignored her.

'Have you found it – or have you been wasting your time gossiping? If that lad of yours has been borrowing my things again, I'll have something to say to him.'

He was gone, stamping up the stairs as if to impose his will on every feeble creaking tread. Poor wilting Mrs Garson wept.

'What are you looking for? Let me help.'

Mrs Garson transferred the thing she was holding in her left hand to the palm of her right.

'The other one like this,' she said.

It was a cuff-link. After the first shock of recognition Lorna joined in the search for its partner, chiefly for moral support. There could be more than one pair of cuff-links consisting of a square stone of dark red rimmed in gold but as she pushed and sifted and automatically sorted buttons into similar sizes, she was pretty sure that the missing link was not there.

She never heard what Councillor Garson had to say to his stepson and took her revenge for his rudeness by pointing out to an invisible audience that since the cuff-links were his, the councillor must at some time have been frequenting the empty Hammond house for who knew what discreditable purpose. But she didn't believe it. It was much more likely that Roy had plundered his stepfather's stud-box in a flurry one evening, having lost all his own links, or possibly one from every pair.

She had not associated the Hammond house with the secret lovers: on the one occasion when she had been inside she had thought only of the Hammond sons killed in action. But it would be a perfect place for clandestine meetings. The couple she had seen might have left just as she arrived to find the door still unlocked. Roy and Alice?

It was becoming impossible to avoid the conclusion. Yet she shrank from the thought of Roy as the heartless man who had walked away, leaving Alice to her fate. To act in such a way was worse than cowardly: it was inhuman. He wasn't like that. But it was not long before her suspicions were confirmed.

It was an unfailing custom with Mabel Hobcroft to put flowers on her husband's grave on the anniversaries of his birth and death and of their wedding day. They had been married in August, 1893. Lorna approved of the ritual as bringing a touch of poetry to a life otherwise directed by unrelieved common sense. She was sorry and more than willing to deputize when on the anniversary of her nuptial day Aunt Mabel was laid low by a bilious attack.

'You'll be better in a day or two and the flowers will last till then.'

Arriving at the lych-gate with her sheaf of roses, lilies, carnations and gypsophila, she met Roy Moxby. Their paths seemed to cross quite frequently these days. He seemed less miserable. He had smartened up a little and was almost presentable. Three or four years ago he must have been quite attractive. She had to force herself to see in the living breathing man at her side the detestable man in black.

'You look like a bride,' he said.

'Aunt Mabel was the bride, thirty years ago. I believe it was a day like this, warm and sunny.'

'What about a walk?'

'Come and help me with these.'

She waited by her Uncle Arthur's grave while he took the vase to the water butt. She heard his footsteps on the flagged path skirting the church as he disappeared round the corner of the north wall – and immediately came to a halt. She heard his voice raised to an unfamiliar pitch as if he were being strangled. It was not speech: it was a single word. A name?

Before she could move he was back, his face white as death, one hand on the church wall for guidance and support as he walked, as if he had gone blind.

'What on earth. . . ?' She went to the path. He pushed past her. She saw him fumble with the latch of the lych-gate and let him go, half convinced that he was out of his mind. He could be subject to sudden fits of derangement: it would explain a lot of things. Unless. . . .

127

She turned the corner of the north wall and saw what he had seen: a girl sitting on a table tomb. She had her back to the church and faced the Beam Valley so that the first thing he must have seen was her long silken mantle of fair hair reaching almost to the flat top of the tomb. If she had turned her head, as she did now, he must have found the profile familiar as Lorna did – or almost did. She wasn't sure until the girl got down and came towards her.

'That was Mr Moxby,' she said. 'He thought I was Alice.'

She was wearing a white blouse fastened at the neck by an ivory brooch in the shape of a cameo.

'The keepsake,' she said, as Lorna glanced at it. 'I wear it all the time but I wouldn't have forgotten you even without it.' She looked round, at the headstones grey and white, and beyond the wall at the rich foliage of trees in the valley, at the intermittent silver gleam of water – and westward to the dam. 'I haven't forgotten anything,' she said and her eyes for an instant had the glint of steel.

# Chapter 14

The return of Etta Hood was to cause a sensation. Roy Moxby was not the only one to be startled by her resemblance to her sister. It could be Alice, people said, sometimes with a touch of awe. It was uncanny. Alice Hood would never be forgotten so long as her living image could be seen walking about in Canterlow. To be dead and gone was bad enough but it was as if, though dead, Alice Hood had not gone but was still there to remind them of how and why she died. It was some time before Etta could enter a shop without a hush falling.

Whether she resembled her sister in other ways remained to be seen. During her three years in London she had been taken in hand by an aunt who owned a small and select boarding house. Her manners were no longer rudimentary. She had found her tongue and spoke and moved with confidence. But it was the glint of steel that Lorna was to remember from time to time, sensing that Etta's assurance was no mere social accomplishment. Etta had never been concerned with society in any sense. Hers was the assurance of a person who knew what she was doing and could therefore be assumed to have an object in mind.

In their first encounter in the churchyard, any pleasure she might have felt in Etta's transformation was overshadowed by its effect on Moxby. She scarcely knew what to say.

'How long will you be staying?'

'I'm not sure how long.' If she meant to say 'how long it will take' she stopped in time.

'You'll be staying with relatives, I suppose.'

'At present, yes.' She had travelled from London overnight.

'And you came here first?'

'To Alice.' She indicated a green mound between the tomb where she had been sitting and the low wall beyond. 'That's where she is.'

They went nearer. Alice's grave was close to the stile in the wall. On the other side a path led down to the river. Lorna was still holding the sheaf of flowers.

'These were meant for someone else but it doesn't matter. I'd like Alice to have them.'

If only she had realized, called out, run down to pick up the hat, she might have been in time and everything would have turned out differently. Regret, sharper than ever with the grave at her feet, brought tears to her eyes. Etta saw the tears but she took the flowers and knelt to lay them on the grave without a word. Lorna left her there and walked quickly away, head bowed, so that she didn't see the altered look in Etta's eyes.

The resources of the one florist in Canterlow were strained to the limit and beyond by the sudden request for another large and expensive sheaf identical with Mrs Hobcroft's. 'For a friend,' Lorna said. 'I'll wait.'

Her extraordinary lateness for lunch was overlooked in the circumstances.

'Etta Hood! On her own? You didn't ask about her parents? I wonder what brought her back. There's nothing for her here. What is she going to do with herself all day long? That's what a lot of people will be wondering – after what happened to Alice.' According to Aunt Mabel other things besides consumption ran in families, and wherever else Etta Hood was seen during the next few weeks it was not in chapel – or church, which would have been better than nothing, but not much better.

130

What *was* Etta going to do with herself all day long? Lorna had been troubled by the same question and had only too quickly arrived at an answer. Etta had come back to fulfil some purpose connected in some way with Alice who had been the whole world to her. It would be like her to react to the heartbreaking loss in some strange way, to identify herself so closely with the sister she resembled as to appear like Alice resurrected: actually to become Alice, not the quiet pious girl Alice had been but the sort of girl she might have been if she could have risen from the grave – or from Miller's Dam – with a glint of steel in her once innocent eyes.

But looking like Alice would not be enough. Whatever form Etta's mission might take it would be both weird and dangerous. Most likely she had come back to find the man who had ruined her sister in order to ruin him too. Mindful of the man she had just failed to see, Lorna sympathized, until she remembered that the black-clad figure resisting Alice's embrace and the hands wrenching her hands away could have been – must have been – those of Roy Moxby.

It was no longer a question of taking him in hand and licking him into shape but of saving him from his fate in Etta's hands, from some unthinkable humiliation or mental torture such as he had already suffered; or from public hostility such as had ended the life of Ezra Kirk.

The horror of that fatal fall had recently been brought home to her more vividly. She had joined Miss Prior and Miss Ellwood on one of their Saturday afternoon rambles. It was to be a picnic, an ill-fated affair. Having set off in warm sunshine and walked uphill for half an hour under a gradually darkening sky, they were caught on the level ground at the top in a stinging shower: a deluge, and not a sheltering tree in sight.

'The best thing is to keep moving,' Miss Prior said sensibly and they struggled on, heads bowed, hair dripping, cotton dresses – and in Lorna's case paper-thin tussore – clinging to their knees until—

'Hoy! Where d'ye think you're goin', you daft gonniels? Stay where ye are.'

He had materialized without warning about thirty yards away, a thin old man bent with rheumatism yet stumbling towards them.

The daft gonniels stopped and peered at him through slanting rain as he came nearer. He was holding a sack over his head and shoulders; his narrow face was red and angry, his speech so rough that it was hard to make out the words. But their drift was clear enough.

'If ye'd gone on that way,' he pointed, 'it would 'a been the last thing ye ever did. Ye'd 'a been over t'Edge, the three o' ye.'

Their startled silence brought a change of mood. His anger cooled.

'That's where ye'd 'a been. And ye wouldn't 'a been the first to go over. Nay, ye wouldn't 'a been the first.'

'Canter Edge.' Even Miss Prior was shaken. 'Oh, my goodness!'

'Ye can go back t'way ye've come – or take yonder trod.' He pointed to his left. 'And ye can stand in t'stable till it clears up – and mind where ye go.'

He had shuffled off, old Tom the cowman. They had followed to a single-storeyed farmhouse and stood like horses in Ezra Kirk's stable until the sky cleared. There was no need to go back the way they had come. An overgrown cart-road behind the farmhouse led downhill and joined the riverside path from Fordham to Canterlow. They had trudged for a while when the way ahead was darkened again, not by rain clouds but by the immense shadow of Canter Edge. They had stopped to look up the towering rock face to where its black edge cleft the sky – and had watched the curving flight of a solitary raven, small as a sparrow in the vast aerial emptiness.

'It makes you realize,' Lorna began. There was no need to go on. It had actually happened – here. The body of a man had come hurtling down from sky to earth, to lie like carrion close to where they were standing. The white pall of snow had been merciful. But Ruth Kirk was right. In every other way that night was god-forsaken.

If Ezra Kirk had been deliberately done to death, that particular form of execution could not be used again without raising questions about the first. Roy was safe from Canter Edge. But there were other ways – and there was also Etta to be reckoned with. Whether he deserved help or not, he must be warned. Twice she had stood aside in situations where she might have helped. Knowing it to be unreasonable, she still felt guilty of having failed Alice; she could certainly have been kinder to Etta. It was time now to intervene.

The issue was too important to depend on a chance meeting. They must meet to talk and in some suitable place, out of doors and undisturbed since neither of them had privacy at home. She remembered the disused lime-kilns halfway along Fold Lane and wrote to him asking him to meet her there the next day but one. 'It is serious, Lorna. . . .' She folded the note and then lest he should get the wrong impression, rewrote it, ending; 'There's something worrying me. I need to talk to you.'

The rendezvous was well chosen. Stone had been quarried there, leaving an amphitheatre scooped from the hillside and a level floor where carts had been driven in and out. Against the escarpment near the entrance were the kilns, overgrown with ivy and bramble, hemlock and willow herb. Their arches, barely visible through tangled leaves and branches, had an ecclesiastical look suitable for a confession if there was to be one. It was certainly a sanctuary for birds and butterflies.

He was already there, sitting on a pile of stone from one of the crumbling kilns. He had been there for half an hour and came towards her, eager and anxious.

'What's it all about?'

One look was enough, No matter what he had done, she could

not hurt him: he was too vulnerable, too defenceless, too incompetent for villainy. She abandoned the bold straightforward opening she had intended – 'Did you know Alice Hood?' He was already troubled, his first question typical in the self-doubt it revealed.

'What have I done now?'

'I want to tell you something.'

He waved her to his seat and hauled himself on to a ledge of stone. She told him what she had seen from the ridge above the dam: Alice appealing to her lover, weeping at his feet, running in the direction of the dam. It was the first time she had spoken of it. Her lips trembled as she came to the end.

'I didn't know what she was going to do.'

She looked across at him. His face was grim.

'I'd like to kill him,' he said.

The relief was overwhelming. They seemed to her, in defiance of Mosaic Law, the most wonderful words she had ever heard.

'Who was he?' she asked when she could speak calmly.

'I don't know. I wish I did. Why have you brought me here and told me all this?' He was genuinely puzzled. 'I don't know what you're up to, Lorna. You're looking pleased. There doesn't seem much to be pleased about.'

'I thought it might be you. I'm sorry. I also thought that it couldn't possibly be you.'

'Thank you. Thank you very much.'

'Your mother told me that you had suddenly changed. She felt it one Sunday evening. I was sure it must be the evening when I saw Alice. And there were other things. You were so terribly shocked when you saw Etta in the churchyard that it did really seem—'

'Just a minute. You don't understand.' The interruption was abrupt and stern. 'What I saw in the churchyard was Alice alive again when the last time I had seen her she was dead.'

Put like that it was macabre enough to bring a shiver to the spine.

'You saw her in the water?'

'I've gone on seeing her like that ever since, day and night, lying there with her hair twisted round her throat. . . . And her eyes. . . .'

She lay beyond the reeds, which were tall enough for a person to pass without seeing her unless he happened to be an angler unable to walk by water without looking at it. To be loitering in the late sunshine of a summer evening and come suddenly on the drowned body of a friend would shatter the nerves of the most insensitive. For him it was much worse. Shocked out of his senses, he had come to himself almost a mile away with no consciousness of how he got there.

'And you didn't go back?'

'No.' He had turned his head away. 'I didn't do any of the things, I ought to have done. I kept it to myself. She was so lovely. I idolized her. For years, ever since I first saw her, I used to hang about hoping to catch a glimpse of her. Well, that was the last glimpse I had of her, the last terrible glimpse.'

He had first seen her when a lonely boy at the age when fairy tales have been outgrown but not forgotten. The fair-haired goose-girl, the princess in the tower and, in his adolescence the Lily Maid of Astolat, had all been Alice Hood. It had been a secret love, a dream to sustain him in a way of life abhorrent to him. His thoughts of her were interfused with the charm of the countryside. He had all he wanted of Arcadia.

From such a dream no awakening could have been more cruel, no nightmare more hideous than the reality.

'Did she know how you felt about her?'

'She didn't even know I existed and wouldn't have looked at me if she did.' He had done nothing more than try to be in places where he might see her. 'She was too young to have anything to do with men. Besides I wouldn't have known how to behave. You're the first girl I've ever been able to talk to comfortably. Don't turn your back on me, Lorna, however much you despise me.'

'I don't despise you. You dreamed of her, feeling she was beyond your reach. There couldn't be anything wrong in that. Think of all the poetry about longing for the unattainable.'

'A man's reach should exceed his grasp, or what's a heaven for? It's the sort of thing people write in autograph books.' The attempt at mockery failed: the lines pleased him.

'As a matter of fact someone wrote it in mine.' She had forgotten who it was – and remembered later with considerable surprise. 'I can imagine how agonizing it must have been to find her in that dreadful way without warning. But. . . .'

'Why did I sneak away without doing anything about it? At first it was pure shock. But I've been in torture ever since, hating myself, trying to explain it to myself. So far as I can remember, once I had taken it in and realized that I was alone there with her like that, I was afraid of being found. I had some idea that people might think I was responsible and hadn't tried to save her. Yes, it was crazy and I've been punished for it by thinking "Suppose she wasn't quite dead. Suppose I could have revived her," even though I was sure she was dead. The other thing was that I couldn't bear to speak of it. I didn't want her to be stared at and talked about and dragged down to the level of common gossip. Better to leave her there alone. It was sunset. There were shafts of light like gold on the water and there were flowers. . . .'

How could she fail to sympathize. She knew what it was to be sustained by an impossible love, never to be fulfilled, the loved one forever out of reach.

'And you see, my cowardly instinct was right. You guessed that I had been there and that made you suspicious.'

'I only thought you might have been her lover.'

'There was no chance of that. I didn't really want to be. It was enough to hold her in my mind, not in the flesh. I knew that even if there had been no distance between us, if I tried to make her love me, the spell would have been broken. I would have made a mess of things. I always do.'

136

She waited, letting silence put its seal on his confession before asking, 'Did you ever see her with a man?'

'Never. I did once catch sight of her on the path through the wood, going toward the old Hammond house. She was alone. I made myself scarce. She didn't see me. The next minute she was gone. I heard a door close.'

'She had gone in?'

'There was nowhere else she could be. I've never seen anyone there and the door is usually locked. I had tried it a few times. Needless to say I gave it a wide berth on that particular day in case – well, she must have been meeting someone. But there is another way in.'

He had later found a cellar door, much overgrown and neither locked nor bolted, and had gone in that way in heavy rain to exchange his wet shirt for the dry jersey in his canvas bag. He had gone upstairs. There were signs that one of the rooms had been used. He had felt pretty sick about it and had never tried the door again. In fact he had avoided the place.

'I wonder who has the key?'

He shrugged as though past caring and seemed too dispirited to go on talking except to say, 'You don't know how grateful I am. I've been groping in the dark and you've shown me a chink of light. I could never have hoped to find a friend like you.'

'I don't think there can be many people with a conscience as tender as yours. Remember – you've done nothing wrong unless it's wrong to care too much. Leaving her there did no harm. The harm had already been done when you found her; and you were right about the gossip there would be, even before you knew the kind of trouble she was in. You didn't know, did you?'

'I didn't know then.'

'If I had been – as she was. . . .' – to compare herself with Alice Hood had been from the beginning intuitive: morbid perhaps but inescapable – 'I would have wanted to be left there, alone.' At peace, she thought, in calm water under a summer sky. 'There was nowhere else she wanted to be.' Since he clearly didn't feel like talking, she went on, 'There's something strange about this part of the world. Sometimes it's so beautiful' – she stopped, defeated. They could never be described, those breathless moments when the harmony of earth and sky seemed to have reached such perfection that the only change must be discordant. 'It makes me apprehensive.'

'Fair as a morning in Eden,' he said, 'and as old as sin.'

'Yes. And that reminds me of something Mr Ushart said.' Alone with him she had hung on his words, the rest of the world banished in mist. She had watched his face as Roy was now watching hers, aware of a change in her voice. 'He said that throughout its long history Canterlow had remained cut off and had turned in on itself. He said that it had developed a communal character which revealed itself in times of crisis and could be dangerous.'

'That was quite a lecture he gave you and he must have enjoyed having such an attentive listener. Still there could be something in it. He may have been thinking of Ezra Kirk.'

She remembered that the brazen-voiced Councillor Garson had seen Ezra leaving the cottage. If he chose to speak of it the whole world would hear, his wife and stepson first of all. She wondered what else they had heard.

'What do you really think happened to him?'

'I'm pretty sure he was murdered. Misadventure, they called it.'

The verdict on Alice had been the same: wrong in both cases. His memory of the August evening when he had found Alice was clear in every detail. Amid the confusion of grief and horror there had been the panic-stricken thought that if he were to be suspected of involvement in her death, it would be the same with him as with Ezra Kirk in the previous year. His behaviour had been so irrational that he could scarcely believe it: he must have been out of his mind.

'That was why I thought – if it ever came out that Alice's lover was a local man. . . .'

'You were warning me.' It was said gently without bitterness.

'I couldn't believe that it really was you and I'm thankful beyond words that it was not because whoever it was, if he lived – or still lives in Canterlow, Etta will find him and he need not hope for mercy when she does.'

'Good God! Is she really like that?'

'Etta is like no one else on earth.'

But Lorna rose from her stony seat feeling happier than when she had come. They had talked quietly. The pigeons had come back to coo soothingly from the ash tree overhanging the nearest kiln. Finches explored the tangle of bramble, hazel and thorn. The sun was warm. Irresponsibly she replaced the burden of guilt where it belonged. There was no need to worry about him: he was safe in China, corrupting the unconverted pagans. Even Etta could not reach him there.

'Memory can be a curse.' Roy put into words what she had often felt. 'There's no way of escaping the regret for all the things one didn't do.'

'There's something you can do.' It was an inspiration. 'Nora Webber is at home now. Why don't you go and see her? I happen to know she thinks of you as a friend.'

'She does?'

'She's had a bad time and life isn't going to be easy for her. She needs her friends.'

'I'm glad you told me.' They walked back to the lane.

'I've just realized,' Lorna said. 'We might have met years ago on the evening Alice died. You can't have been far away when I stood on the ridge and saw her.'

'We missed each other by minutes. Together we might have saved her.'

'If only by being there. Still, we were evidently meant to meet one day. By the way, keep on calling at the Hammond house. It may still be there, your stepfather's cuff-link. I put it on the window ledge in the hall.'

'So – in addition to all your other gifts you can work miracles. Let's go there now.'

'You go. I'll be thinking of a way to get it back to its rightful owner without incriminating the person who borrowed it.'

It was indeed a miracle to have made him smile again.

# Chapter 15

Since the signal, brief but momentous, which had passed between the two people mist-bound on the Gorsham road, Lorna had kept away from the schoolhouse. Her visits had been to an invalid; Madeline's health was improving; the family could withdraw into its former seclusion; she would not be missed.

She was wrong in both conclusions.

'You have deserted me.' The note was brief. 'I looked forward to your visits. Will you not drop in again as you used to? Madeline.' She had added a postscript written less clearly. 'Please come, Lorna.'

Tilly, who had delivered the note, was still in the kitchen having a word with Gladys.

'You will come, won't you, miss? She could do with a bit of cheering up.' And when Lorna called at the schoolhouse an hour later, Tilly came out into the porch to whisper though no one else could possibly have heard: 'She's ill in bed now and has been for best part of a month. There's something inside of her that they can't do anything about. You go up and talk to her like you used to do.'

'I'm very sorry. Mrs McNab should have let me know.'

'Mrs McNab isn't here to let anybody know anything. She took and packed her bags a fortnight yesterday and went back to Scotland.'

'So there's only you? You need help, Tilly, and Mrs Ushart needs company.'

'There's help and company of a sort such as it is,' Tilly said darkly.

The bedroom was large, long and dim, unaltered in its dimensions since the days when the schoolhouse was also the school and boys from outlying farms came as boarders. The big brass bedstead was opposite the door so that she saw Madeline directly and was dismayed by the change in her.

'I'm glad you've come.' She was gaunt from loss of flesh, pallid as the pillows and so weak that without their support, Lorna felt, she must surely lie down and never rise again. The black hair had lost its sheen: the blue eyes, large in their now cavernous setting, had the strange lustre sometimes to be seen in the eyes of the dying. Between pity for her suffering and sadness at the sight of rare beauty wasting away, Lorna could not trust herself to speak.

The first shock was swiftly followed by astonishment.

'You may go, Etta.'

She had been standing in the embrasure by the window, partly concealed by a curtain, unnoticed in the dimness of the room, and now came quietly to the bed. She wore a white apron and had her hair 'up'. Her murmured 'Miss Kent' with lips pursed and an accompanying nod suggested a companionship in realizing the gravity of the situation. She took a tray from the bedside table and left, carefully closing the door.

'How long has Etta been here?' Lorna found her tongue.

'Two or three weeks. You know her?'

'She was a pupil.'

'She needed work and somewhere to stay. My husband felt that a girl like her, and on her own, needed protection.'

There was no girl like Etta. Nevertheless so far as could be seen, the room was immaculate: she was evidently competent. How like Adam to take on the responsibility of looking after her!

She did need protection, though from what it was not easy to envisage.

'Not much personality,' Madeline was saying, 'and very little to say, but useful, especially since Monica McNab decided to leave.'

'Why did she leave?'

'She had her reasons I suppose.' They were evidently not to be discussed. 'I particularly wanted to see you. There's no one else I can talk to.'

'I thought as you seemed better. . . . If I'd known you were ill I would certainly have come.'

Madeline raised a fleshless hand as if to interrupt.

'I know why you stayed away. It was to avoid seeing him, wasn't it? You need not feel guilty. I don't mind.' She spoke slowly, drawing difficult breaths. 'Adam has great charm. Who should know that better than his wife?' The smile that accompanied the words made them ambiguous. 'From the beginning I guessed that you would find him irresistible – as he can be. He is not easy to please but I have wondered if he found you irresistible too.'

'No. Certainly not. He has never. . . . We have never. . . .' She broke off. The word 'we' suggested a relationship. 'You mustn't speak of such a thing or even think it.'

'I'm sorry, but remember, it's because I trust you that I can speak to you like this.'

Her speech was slurred and slow but there was as much directness in her manner as her weakness would allow and unmistakable sincerity in her eyes, which had sometimes seemed more watchful than expressive. Lorna's impression during those earlier visits was confirmed: much had been left unsaid. She too had something to conceal. Now, at the eleventh hour, it was as if no time must be wasted either through tact or deception.

'He would not be the first to find you attractive, I'm sure, and yet you've never mentioned any young man as most girls of your age might do when talking confidentially with an older woman. There is no one?'

Lorna shook her head and wished she hadn't come.

'Please, you said it was important.'

'What will become of him, a widowed schoolmaster with two young children? I cannot die in peace for the thought of leaving them to a housekeeper – or worse.' For the first time she showed distress, turning her head from side to side, her face twisted.

'You're in pain?' Lorna looked helplessly at the various bottles on the bed-table.

'In agony when I think of my children.' With a tremendous effort she contrived to sit up and lean forward. 'You must help, Lorna. You love children and Paul and Amy love you. They know you. It would be easy for you to love their father if you don't already. He wouldn't be able to help loving you. You're the kind of girl men love for the right reasons. Marry him when I'm gone – and soon. Promise.'

'How could I possibly promise such a thing? You must trust him to do what is best for the children. He always does, for everybody's children. He will make his own decisions.'

'But suppose he makes the wrong one. A man can be misled – by inclinations you know nothing about – and plunge himself and others into misery.' She fell back and feebly indicated a box of tablets. 'They're for the pain.'

'You're talking too much.' Lorna poured water into a glass and held it as she sipped.

'I do understand. . . . So much difference in your ages. . . . But not so much. . . !'

'I'll do anything else, Madeline. I can promise that.'

'Get Monica back. Make her come back.'

She closed her eyes. Lorna adjusted the pillows and laid her back to rest. She had been in no state to concern herself even about so vital a matter as the future of those she was leaving behind. Nothing could be more natural but the agitation had been too much for her. She lay with eyes closed but not in peace. There were spells of murmuring, the words barely audible. From her recent experience of nursing Aggie, Lorna knew how narrow a line there could be between consciousness and delirium: how the sufferer could wander the dark corridors of the mind and return, not to safety but to renewed awareness of pain and subjection to the numberless discomforts of the failing body. But in that twilight state Aggie had not been tormented as Madeline was by some deep-rooted distress rigorously controlled in normal life.

Listening unhappily to the disjointed words, she heard the theme of their recent talk repeated, with constant reference to ages: 'The difference in their ages. . . . So much younger. . . . Not half his age. . . .' She waited for a few minutes and presently the muttering ceased. After a little hesitation she left, feeling that she herself had aged since entering the room.

As she closed the door after her, the invalid opened her eyes. The distress of mind and body seemed to have left her to less untranquil thoughts, their drift impossible to know. She was herself again. Nothing she had said betrayed the wry satisfaction she felt in having done her best to gain for him what he wanted or ought to want, in spite of knowing as she did what can come from getting what one wants: she had wanted him so much. And there would be the same risk for little Miss Kent. That would be a shame but the children need not suffer; whereas if he should make a different choice. . . . A man could lose his head over a seventeen-year-old girl with consequences not to be thought of. She would not think of them. The merciful opiate was taking effect. She drifted into sleep.

Adam was waiting in the hall when Lorna went down.

'Thank you for coming. How did she seem to you?'

'She asked for one of her tablets. I hope it was right to give it to her. She was in some pain. I stayed until she fell asleep.'

He happened to stand in a dusty shaft of sunlight from the hall window. She had allowed herself a swift glance and did not look again. Once had been enough. She had expected to see him looking strained, weary, even ill but she could not have foreseen how deeply dispirited he would seem, standing in the golden mote-filled light as if to darken it.

'Did she talk to you?' She thought he asked anxiously, wondering no doubt if Madeline had spoken of some discomfort she had concealed from him.

'A little but she really wasn't well enough to talk.'

'Excuse me.' Etta had appeared with a jug of hot water, a clean cloth folded over it. They stood aside as she went softly upstairs.

'What a change in her!' Lorna could not help saying. 'It did her good to go away for a while – and she must feel safe here. She was so unhappy.'

'You'll come again?' It was no more than an enquiry, in no way persuasive, and Lorna felt no obligation to answer. He nodded as if he understood and went into his study.

There was no need for her to stay, yet she was strangely reluctant to leave and went slowly to the foot of the stairs, in response to some compulsion purely instinctive. On the third step she saw Etta coming down and turned back: it was unlucky to pass on the stairs. Etta smiled and vanished into the kitchen.

She was free to go up, at every step less conscious of reality: of her hand on the unsteady stair-rail, her feet on the worn carpet, aware as never before of a relentlessness in the passage of time and the significance, in all its vastness, of every fleeting second and especially – for some reason - of this very moment.

Madeline seemed to be asleep. The quietness and perfect order of the room should have been reassuring. From the doorway she looked again at the most beautiful face she had ever seen. It was ravaged by suffering, yet her impression was of its haunting loveliness. She went to the bed, stooped and kissed the white brow. No word was spoken but whether in appeal – or regret – there came a change of expression; a tremor of eye-lids; a hand feebly raised as if reaching out for the true friendship that had escaped them.

She never saw Madeline again; and when in years to come she recalled the hours they had spent together, it was in the light of knowledge undreamed of at the time.

# Chapter 16

The news of Mrs Ushart's death was not unexpected: she had been in poor health ever since she had come to Canterlow. Few had known her personally. To refer to her as 'poor Mrs Ushart' was as near as most people could come to grieving for her. The wave of sympathy that rocked the town was for Mr Ushart. His reputation, always high, had never been higher. It was right and proper that he should be overcome by his sad loss and anyone could see suffering written all over him.

Lorna saw it in the deepening lines of his thin face and the absent look in his eyes; she was aware of hesitation in his normally quick movements and speech. He had always been firmly in charge, positive, decisive. She had not expected to see him downcast as if he had ceased to be master of circumstances and become their victim. She almost felt, though she suppressed the feeling, that his suffering was disproportionate to even so profound a bereavement as a husband must endure in losing his wife.

But the face like that of an artist or a poet was of a kind to withstand its loss of colour and animation without losing one iota of its magnetism – at least for one of the more besotted of his admirers.

Inevitably in the weeks after Madeline's death she saw him more often. The funeral had been a private affair. The three or four distant relatives who came had left without even staying the night. The bewildered children were looked after at The Birches for a few days. Mrs Hobcroft felt that it was the least she could do: and Lorna must not be popping in and out of the schoolhouse. 'Not now,' she said. 'It wouldn't be suitable.'

Instead their father called for them occasionally to take them out and to hear how splendid it was at Mrs Hobcroft's; how Miss Kent had said this or that; had read them bedtime stories; taught them to play Snap and Happy Families and shown them pictures of America where her father lived.

'Miss Kent won't go to America, will she?' Amy asked. 'I don't want her to.'

'Don't be silly,' Paul said. 'She's sure to want to see her father and I expect she'd come back. This is where she lives.'

If it was unsuitable for Lorna to pop in and out of the school-house, how could it be suitable for the headmaster to be left to the dubious ministrations of such a couple as Tilly and Etta Hood? Obviously Etta must go.

'You've been very good, taking her in,' Mrs Hobcroft told him, 'but she can't stay without an older woman in the house.'

'I'll speak to her,' he said absently. 'There are so many problems.'

'Things can't go on in the same way, Etta,' Lorna told her when she called one morning at The Birches with clothes for the children. 'I'm afraid you'll have to leave.'

'Of course. Mr Ushart has only to say the word and I'll try to find somewhere else to stay.'

She had let her hair down again and looked younger. Very young. The morning air had not brought colour to her cheeks but in contrast to their strange whiteness her blue eyes and crimson lips were flower-like and vivid. Her hair, flowing in a shining cascade to her waist, seemed imbued with a separate life of its own. Her appearance was arresting.

Lorna was pleased to find her so co-operative. It was an opportunity to raise the question of Mrs McNab.

'Do you know why she left?'

'No. But then I hardly knew her. I was here for just a few days before she left.' Etta spoke freely, apparently innocent of at least one conclusion to be drawn from so brief an acquaintance and so abrupt a departure.

After informal discussions between the headmaster and the School Board it was decided that Mrs McNab should be asked to return and that under the circumstances, to make things easier for Mr Ushart, someone else should write. Mrs Hobcroft offered to do so. Together she and Lorna concocted the letter. Mrs McNab replied by return of post. She would come at once if only for the sake of the children but not while Etta Hood was there.

'Thank goodness for that.' Aunt Mabel passed the letter to Lorna. 'Etta Hood simply must go. She has relatives, cousins or something of the sort, and can go to them. I wonder why Mrs McNab can't stand having her there. You said she looked after Mrs Ushart quite nicely.'

A month later Etta was still there. Mrs McNab was adamant. So, in a different way, was Mr Ushart.

'I took the girl in and I refuse to be influenced by the threat of small-town gossip, nor can I allow decisions to be taken for me by others. People must mind their own business as I shall mind mine. Until she finds other work and somewhere else to live, she stays. The girl has morbid tendencies and may be tempted to end her own life as her sister did. There are other housekeepers besides Mrs McNab.'

He was speaking to the managers who had met again unofficially at The Birches. Lorna, bringing in coffee, heard him and rejoiced. He sounded more like himself and he was right to stand his ground. It was for such integrity that he was admired in the town. Yet he did not look himself. He was not happy in voicing his scruples. He was both weary and, she thought, agitated.

'It is a matter of principle.' His voice broke.

'Principle?' boomed Councillor Garson. 'It should be a matter of common sense. If Ushart can't be reasonable, there's only one thing to do. Offer the woman McNab more money and she'll come. Money talks. What were you paying her, Ushart?'

They were torturing him. The descent to pounds, shillings and pence was positively sickening. Lorna deliberately omitted to offer the Councillor a cup of coffee, regretting her inability to remove him from the face of the earth.

'Surely that is a private matter.' Aunt Mabel alone was undaunted by the Councillor's massive awfulness. The others had shrunk from it as they appeared also to have shrunk in size.

'Mr Ushart is doing what he feels to be a Christian duty,' the vicar said in mild defiance. 'I think a housekeeper might be found by means of an advertisement in *The Church Times* – and I should be happy to see to it myself if all are agreeable. Mr Ushart?'

He nodded. There was a general murmur of agreement, coffee was drunk and the managers left.

'A churchgoer,' Aunt Mabel said. 'We may as well resign ourselves.'

Councillor Garson clapped a restraining hand on the headmaster's shoulder as the others dispersed in the street. 'I want a word with you. You'll have heard about Birkett over at Maywick?'

Ushart was immediately attentive. Birkett was the headmaster whose retirement or demise would leave vacant the headship he had long coveted.

'What about Birkett?'

'He's had a heart attack. Not fatal. They say he's pulling round. He'll be given sick leave for six months and he might hang on a bit after that. But he might not. One heart attack can lead to another. We might even have to make a temporary appointment which could become permanent.'

'I hadn't heard.'

'I told you what I'd be prepared to do – a bit too much considering what you did for me.'

'And am still doing,' Ushart said curtly. The notion of a bargain with this brute had disgusted him from the start. He looked round uneasily. Garson had lowered his voice by a decibel or two but it was still loud. Fortunately there was no one about.

'Well, we'll say no more about that. It suits me to have him where he can have an eye kept on him. God knows he needs it. And it keeps his mother from whining all the time.'

'And the Maywick business?'

'Look here, I'll tell you to your face what I wouldn't say behind your back. The committee will never appoint a widower with a young family. I'll never be able to bring them round to it. You'll need to find a wife – and not waste too much time about it.'

'How can you speak like that, man, with my wife not cold in her grave?'

His impulse was to walk off and have no more truck with this bloated upstart; and he did actually turn away, just long enough to be aware of the narrow street closing him in: the eager gossip behind lace curtains; the problems awaiting him at home whose complexity he alone knew; the desperate need to break away from it all before it was too late.

In Maywick he could begin again. The prospect had sustained him for years; the trials of his personal life would have been unbearable without the hope of escape. Madeline's final act of revenge had been to die too soon.

With the prize almost within his grasp, he could not let it go. To leave Canterlow had ceased to be a hope, a dream: it had recently become an absolute necessity.

'You'd best look about you. You won't have any difficulty.' The elephantine coyness of the man was as humiliating as a dig in the ribs. 'There's plenty of young women that wouldn't say no to a chap like you. Only wish I had the chance. Anyway, I've given you fair warning.'

Time passed. *The Church Times* produced two or three applicants but no housekeeper was appointed. Mrs McNab remained in Scotland, Etta at the schoolhouse. A possible solution to the problem came from an unexpected quarter.

The Cutlers' Ball in Donnerton was an annual affair, an event of some prestige. Cedric had invited Lorna months ago. She and Aunt Mabel would spend a few days at High Croft. The Ball was to be on a Friday. Cedric came to fetch them the day before. Having taken a day off he had time to see a little more of Canterlow than had been possible on his two former visits. Lorna showed him the sights: the Castle; the old prison, now disused, being far too small; the medieval wall paintings in the church. . . .

'There's an olde-world feeling about places like this,' he remarked, not surprisingly, as they turned into Abbot's Lane, 'as if time stood still and hasn't really started again. You get the feeling of things lying under the surface, like wrecks under the sea.'

'Yes, I believe it is like that.' She smiled at his astuteness. 'And this is the school.'

'A pretty little place. And the old fellow standing in the doorway. Is that the headmaster?'

'Cedric! Mr Ushart isn't old.' She was deeply shocked, troubled too. Adam had a worn look these days and he had seemed just now to stoop a little as if hesitating whether to go or stay.

He had hesitated on their account, having caught sight of them as they passed: Lorna with a rather fine-looking young fellow. She was looking up at him and smiling – saw Adam and waved.

'Sorry. Middle-aged.' Cedric wondered why she had been so put out. 'Not much more than early forties, I should say.'

'His wife died recently.' For some reason she found herself telling him about the difficulties at the schoolhouse: the housekeeper refusing to work with Etta; the headmaster refusing to be bullied into acting against his principles; the children. 'We often have them at The Birches.'

'We have that sort of trouble at the works from time to time: man refusing to work with somebody who knocked him down the night before; women squabbling about how to make tea. The thing is to compromise. Try to arrange it so that neither side feels the other has won. Meet both parties halfway. The Scottish lady is keen to come. He should get her here on the understanding that it's only for the time being and offer a few concessions. I take it there'd be much less work, for instance, with no invalid and two young women in the house.'

'He could let her have Madeline's room.' Lorna warmed to the idea. 'It's big enough to be a sitting-room as well as a bedroom. I think it used to be a dormitory.'

'She needn't see much of this Etta. What's wrong with her, by the way? Never mind. She can be told to mind her p's and q's. She'll behave herself if she thinks it's a temporary arrangement. It's more than likely they'll settle down together.'

'You're the most sensible person I know, Cedric.'

'Oh, I don't know. You live and learn, that's all.'

But he had always known what to do. She was reminded of a day at the seaside when they were children. The crowded beach had confused her. Running to retrieve a ball, she had lost sight of the others and stood terrified among strangers by the unfamiliar sea until all at once Cedric was there. 'Don't go that way, Lorna,' he said. 'You'll get lost,' and he had taken her by the hand and led her back to safety.

They called at Abbey Farm for eggs and passed the school again as they strolled home for lunch.

'One thing I have learned,' Cedric said. 'Always be suspicious of people who do things on principle. It sometimes means that they want to do it and don't like to say so, or they do it because they have no choice. Isn't it going a bit too far to keep the girl on and lose the older woman who would make a home for the children?'

\*

155

Lorna's dress of cream satin with beaded panels, worn with a beaded headband, was equal to anything Donnerton could produce.

'Even if I am a country bumpkin,' she said, when the Liffeys told her how well she looked.

'They danced together as children,' Dora Liffey murmured as Cedric helped Lorna into her squirrel coat.

'A lot of things have happened since then.' Mabel Hobcroft's headshake was ominous. 'There are things Lorna keeps to herself.'

'It's the same with Cedric.'

Both Lorna and Cedric enjoyed the dancing.

'You've improved,' Lorna said. 'You used to lumber.'

'So have you. You used to be too stiff.'

He introduced his friends: fellow cutlers; members of the Music Society; the co-founder of the club the two of them had formed for crippled boys; the curator of the Art Gallery and his wife. She and Lorna had been at school together. The Ball and indeed the whole weekend were delightfully free of problems. Lorna reproved herself for having slid in recent months into a state of mind troubled by anxieties, some of them undefined, none of her own seeking. In future she would lead a life of her own and enjoy it. They returned home on Sunday.

The next day Adam asked her to be his wife.

# Chapter 17

A wood can be alluring in summer when thick foliage limits the view: in winter it offers no escape from reality. Naked boughs let in too much light; there are no shadows, only shapes clearly outlined against a cold sky.

More than once Lorna's slow walk dragged to a halt. When the regular crunch of fallen leaves ceased, there came in its place a lull of such intensity that it threatened, like a challenge demanding an answer. The combination of utter stillness and merciless light made evasion impossible. She walked on again as if in motion she might come to a decision.

It had become an obsession. There could be no other word for her concentration beyond all reason on one idea: an inward activity so compelling that her response to the familiar outer world had been stultified; she had been only half-awake, partially blind. The wonderful thing had happened. Years of longing had ended in fulfilment: he had told her that he loved her; that she alone could make him happy; she would be the ideal wife every man longed for. She loved him: he alone could make her happy. It was a situation to make any normal woman triumphant, soberly grateful, ecstatically happy, ardent in showing her love, eager to be caressed – according to the kind of woman she was. But it wasn't like that.

Perhaps it had happened too suddenly. It had been, as it

had always been, the very last thing she expected. She was still far from realizing that her devotion had depended on the distance between them: it could be free to quicken and burgeon because nothing would ever have to be done about it: there was no foreseeable end to it. Had she not told herself in all sincerity that it was harmless, her own secret, offering no threat to Madeline or the children or to him? She had recognized the similarity between Roy's adoration of Alice Hood and her own infatuation. Both flourished in an unreal state of existence like the island of the lotus-eaters where no responsible action was required. The feeling could therefore be indulged as an opiate.

Too sudden and certainly in the wrong place. There was nowhere else they could be alone. He had waylaid her as she left the schoolhouse after bringing the children home from The Birches. 'Please, I must speak to you.' She had gone with him through the twilit garden to the school, her heart thumping. It was nearly dark in the hall. He had lowered the blinds – in preparation. And afterwards – 'You need a little time,' he said, kissing her hand as they parted.

Since then she had scarcely slept. After days and nights of honest thinking she had succeeded in separating the lotus-induced dream from the immediate reality, the offer of marriage by a highly respected man of many talents and a promising future whose every attribute she admired and for years had loved. She would be mistress in her own home at last.

She congratulated herself on being capable of taking a rational view and was immediately aware that there were rational drawbacks. The home would not be hers: it would be Madeline's with Madeline's children in it, and also the incalculable Etta whom Adam was keeping there on principle. At that point she failed to remember Cedric's interpretation of the word. If Adam should be promoted to another school at

Maywick (exchanging a faulty geyser for a reliable hot water system, she recalled with a touch of hysteria) Madeline's influence might fade. Distanced from the green sofa, the long dark bedroom and windows from which little could be seen but the reflection of one's own anxious face looking out, she would have a home of her own. But in the immediate future. . . .

'It would be too soon,' she had emerged from her confusion to protest, 'for you to marry again. What would people think?'

They would think so speedy a marriage indicated either an attachment formed before Madeline's death or the practical need of a stepmother for the children.

'The only thing that matters is that I love you,' he said and took her in his arms and kissed her as she had sometimes longed for him to do, secure in the knowledge that it would never happen.

She stopped and leaned against the moss-green trunk of an ash tree, grateful for its strength and indifference to human folly. Something was wrong. Despite Aunt Mabel's convictions that she was not the marrying kind, Lorna had thought quite as much about marriage and on the same lines as most young women. One married for love. Pros and cons were secondary to the rapture of mutual love. With no experience of love-making, perhaps because of that, instinct told her that there was something wrong with the kiss. It lacked tenderness. It had not made her feel that she was, as he said, a woman dearly loved. It was the kiss of a man deeply engrossed in graver concerns. Something had happened to make her feel a distance between them which had not existed when intimacy was forbidden. Separated from him by the barrier of convention, she had felt only their closeness. Now it was as if the barrier had fallen, leaving them free to stare at each other across a gap neither found it easy to cross.

His preoccupation must be with Madeline. What else could

it be? A second wife must always feel behind her the shadow of the first. How could a wife so beautiful – of so subtle and pervasive a character as Madeline – ever be replaced except by a useful, dutiful woman never in any sense to be considered as her equal?

Yet she felt instinctively that the change in Adam was not due entirely to the loss of Madeline, though what other cause there might be she could not imagine. If some additional problem tormented him at such a difficult time in his life, he would need help and companionship. Come to think of it, he didn't seem to have any close friends. She thought of herself with contempt. After loving him for years, why was she hesitating? He had offered himself. What more could he offer? What more did she want? It was concern for him that made a refusal impossible.

'You'll think about it?' he had pleaded, the pleading more urgent than the kiss. 'But don't keep me too long in suspense, Lorna. I need you more than anything in the world.' She had promised to think it over and left him, her retreat undignified and, she now felt, ungracious.

She roused herself, parted reluctantly from the ash tree and went on. It was a long time since she had come this way. Faced with the most important decision of her life, she was weary in mind and spirit and needed to be alone. No one ever came here. The house was already in sight, its twin gables more clearly visible than in summer when thickly mantled with clinging vines. The Hammond house. It must surely have a more impressive name; and yet, aloof in its solitude, it gave so strong an impression of existing in its own right and on its own terms that it needed neither name to identify it nor any clear address since it belonged neither to Canterlow nor to Fordham a mile further west.

This time she was approaching the house from the opposite direction, having taken the shorter way through the churchyard, across a bridge near the mill and by a series of narrow paths to the wood. She came out into a clearing about fifty yards from the house and for the first time saw on her left a path leading to the green slope above the dam. If Roy was right in assuming that the lovers had made use of the house, that was the way they would very likely take. They had probably left just before she arrived on that first fateful evening.

Forgetful for a while of her own affairs, she felt only the fascination of the place: an empty house with a tragic history; haunt of ill-fated lovers; close to the scene of a fourth untimely death. She had not thought of it in quite that way before as if the house itself were doomed.

She pushed open the gate, approached the front door and found it unlocked as it had been that other time. The two could actually have been here when she left Fold Lane: a few minutes earlier she might have surprised them to the embarrassment of all three. And yet since every event affects the one that follows, her arrival might have altered the design and might conceivably have saved a life.

She cautiously pushed the door open and waited, listening. She had suddenly remembered the cuff-link. It would take only seconds to slip in no further than the nearest window ledge. Even if there was someone in the house, she would not be heard. A glance was enough. The cuff-link had gone.

The house was cold, the huge grate black. The atmosphere was as sepulchral in its silence as before, her mood nervous and superstitious. But having ventured in, convinced that she had the place to herself, she might as well explore a little. Besides, why should she mind being found there? Whoever was responsible for the place should keep it locked.

Several rooms opened off the hall: an oak-panelled dining room; a drawing-room with tarnished brass candle sconces on its white walls; a small room once snug, no doubt, with books and a wood fire, now dark and damp. Unable to resist the impulse, she climbed the stairs. There were bedrooms on either side of a long landing, all empty of furniture except the one nearest the stair-head. A bed – a chair. . . . Her quick look round coincided with sounds below: the closing of the door; the firm tread of heavy boots on the flagged floor.

# Chapter 18

They stared at each other, she at the top of the staircase, he at the bottom.

'Good God! You frightened the life out of me.'

He was young, fair-haired, arrested in the act of pulling off the topmost of several sweaters.

'I'm sorry.' She came down three steps. 'I have absolutely no right to be here.' Then recovering her wits, 'Have you?'

'Any right to be here? In strictly legal terms, yes. Morally speaking, probably not. What right has either of us to be here, considering. . . .' He had pulled off the sweater and draped it on the newel post. He was no longer looking at her but round the hall – or was it into the space between stairs and fireplace? – with faint bewilderment.

'Considering those who aren't here? I feel that too.' It was true. The presence in the stricken house of two young and healthy people did seem an intrusion on the privacy of the dead.

'You knew them?' He looked at her with more interest.

'No, no. I only came to live in Canterlow after the war but of course I know about the family who lived here.' She had come down to his level. He was fresh complexioned, blue-eyed. 'I certainly should not have been peering into other people's rooms – like Goldilocks. I was going anyway even if you hadn't come.'

'I believe she was quite kindly treated when the bears came home.' He had brought in a bag of logs and a bundle of kindling and now dragged them to the fireplace. 'As a matter of fact you're welcome to stay. The place feels different with a fire and I could do with company.' Especially the company of the sort of girl she seemed to be: quiet-voiced, graceful, self-possessed but not assertive and certainly good to look at.

'Is there any paper to get it going?'

'In my room.'

She raked out ash with a rusted poker while he fetched a newspaper.

'I'm Lorna Kent.'

'Julian Hammond,' and seeing that she was taken aback, 'a cousin.'

They knelt on the bare floor watching the paper then the twigs ignite.

'You're staying here?'

'For a few days. Leaving tomorrow. It's not too cheerful. Actually you're the first person I've spoken to since I left the station at Canterlow on Saturday.' He seemed all at once boyish and low-spirited. She had known at once that there was nothing to fear from him: that he was in some way lost, a feeling she could share.

'I don't suppose there's a chair.'

'In the kitchen.' He looked more cheerful. 'I'll fetch it. The legs are firm. Can't answer for the back. What about a cup of tea?'

He also brought a Primus stove, a kettle of water, cups and a metal teapot and sat on a dry sack, his head under the mantelpiece, his long legs stretched on the hearthstone, until the kettle boiled.

'The simple life.' He handed her a dark brew in an enamel cup. 'There's nothing like it.'

'Nothing.' Lorna grimaced at her first sip of milkless tea.

Despite his casual confidence of manner, she sensed in him as they talked a darker mood: a disillusioned bitterness. This was his territory yet he was no more in possession than she was. A young man living, if only for a short time, in an empty house with no neighbours but trees must either be reclusive by nature or in hiding or – as she suspected – there against his will.

'You were right about the fire,' she said. 'It does make a difference.' The logs had taken hold and were throwing out a crimson light. Presently she felt a faint warmth on her cold feet and on her face. 'I have been here before. Once.' She told him about the apples. 'Aunt Mabel was afraid they would go to waste. We left the next day and I never heard whether she found someone to gather them for her. Would it have been stealing?' She remembered that the door had been unlocked then too. 'Do you come here often?'

'Only now and then.' When the war ended he had no fixed occupation. He was acting temporarily as agent for his aunt, mother of the three boys who died. She was now a widow living in Sussex and had engaged him to look after the property in Canterlow until she could make up her mind what to do with it.

'It must have been a lovely place once – and could be still.'

She recreated the hall for him, first having had the place thoroughly cleaned: no suits of armour or stags' heads but comfortable chairs with chintz covers; Indian rugs; (no tiger-skins) amber-shaded lamps; a table against the panelled wall to the right of the stairs.

'It's a hobby,' she confessed, 'to furnish houses in my mind. It comes from always having lived in other people's.'

'You too?'

Later she heard more of his history. His parents had separated when he was ten. After that his home was here at Canterlow with his father's brother, Colonel Hammond and his wife. He became part of the family, went to the same school as his cousins and would have volunteered for active service as they did.

165

'But they wouldn't have me. My mother is German and that made me a risk from the point of view of security especially as her family had military connections. My grandfather had served under the command of General Count Helmuth von Moltke, Chief of German General Staff – and since the separation she has been living in Germany. It was thought that my sympathies would be divided or even pro-German.'

And were they, she wondered. Without supposing him to be capable of treachery, she felt that the most straightforward thing about him was his appearance. His fair hair, blue eyes, athletic figure and ease of movement qualified him as the hero in an adventure story for boys. His smile could be winning, she thought, but it could also be mocking and self-derogatory. Deep in his heart and mind there must have been conflict. His loyalty to Britain could have been half-hearted. On the other hand she had read that converts to a faith were often more devout because they had not been born into it. Was he at heart even more British than the Hammond boys and consequently dangerously embittered by being debarred from the army?

She was ashamed of so wary an attitude when he told her that he had volunteered as a stretcher-bearer for one of the Quaker relief organizations.

'So you saved lives instead of ending them.'

'It didn't feel like that when I was eighteen.'

She had been right. He had never recovered from the official rebuff.

The hall where they sat, the rooms around and above were all unpeopled except for themselves and their own shadows thrown by firelight on the bare walls. In other circumstances he might have been more reticent but they talked with the freedom of strangers, more at ease than if they had known each other for years. At first his references to the family were brief but gradually he evoked for her the carefree days before the war. She listened absorbed, sharing his memories in the very place where they must be most vivid; feeling, as he must feel, regret for a lost world and a way of life gone for ever.

'I wonder if your aunt realizes what it means to you to come back.'

This had been his refuge from a background into whose accepted pattern he didn't quite fit. Neither did she. From birth she had been unlike girls who had fathers and mothers living together in close-knit families. His parents' separation and his divided nationhood must have had a similar effect on him, intensified by the war in which his parents ranked as enemies.

With the four boys home for the holidays the house had burst into life. She imagined the racket of doors slammed, the enormous meals, the busy servants. One Christmas the dam had been frozen. They had skated, singly and in pairs: George and Leonard; Digby and Julian, the youngest. He had shared a room with Digby who was a year older, the room he was using now. Then it had been crammed with trophies: a fox's brush; cases of birds' eggs and butterflies; photographs of cricket XI's and groups of the Officers' Training Corps.

They used the apple tree under their window to come and go though there wasn't the slightest need: they could come and go through the front door whenever they liked: Aunt Beatrice never fussed. Uncle George was usually in his library. He was Colonel of the County Yeomanry and a student of military history. But he joined them to play with the toy fort when they were younger and could be relied on for detailed accounts of incidents on the Northwest Frontier: the Charge of the Light Brigade; the battle at Rorke's Drift when a hundred South Wales Borderers withstood attack by thousands of Zulu warriors.

'All that was history. We couldn't hear enough of it. The real thing was different.'

George had been killed in October 1914 in the defence of the Ypres salient by the British 1st Corps, outnumbered 2–1. Six months later Leonard died in the spring offensive of the second

battle of Ypres. Digby was one of thousands mown down by enemy gunfire on the first morning of the battle of the Somme in 1916.

She guessed from his manner that the loss of Digby had been the worst blow.

'You were very close.'

'They called us David and Jonathan, closer than brothers.' He put another log on the fire, taking a little time over it. 'That's why I can't forgive myself for letting him go without putting things right.'

'Had you quarrelled?'

'Once. The first and last time.'

The row had blown up suddenly on the last day of his leave. They had gone to bed, still furious, without speaking to each other. When Julian woke next morning, Digby had gone – had crept away so as not to wake him. He found a note: 'Goodbye, old chap.' A fortnight later Digby was dead.

'How terrible for you!' The sympathy in her voice startled him.

'You understand how I felt? How I've gone on feeling?'

'I do. Somehow it's always too late to put things right. But it must have been about something very important to you both – the quarrel, I mean.'

'Important! It was the most trivial thing in the world – a row about something neither of us cared twopence for. Digby gave me a dressing-down for messing about, as he called it, with a local girl. It wasn't done, he said. God knows what he imagined I had done. There was nothing in it, nothing at all. She came here once or twice with the old man who cleaned and oiled the clocks, her father or grandfather. Can't even remember her name. She was pretty with long fair hair and I was rather taken with her looks. But I tell you, when I read that note I hated her. I hate the very thought of that girl. She got in the way and came between Digby and me. She ruined my life.'

'You mustn't let her.' He was being absurd as well as being

unjust. 'Don't let anything ruin your life. That would make the whole thing even more of a waste – the only one of you left living to have nothing to live for? It doesn't make sense.'

'Nothing makes sense.'

In the summer of 1916 Colonel and Mrs Hammond had left: the house was cleared, discarded like an empty shell. He was the only one who had come back once or twice in search of consolation, only, she imagined, to be made more miserable, hearing the voices of the dead. Later he had come to keep an eye on the property and to see the woodman about the timber.

The short winter afternoon had waned. The windows were now red with reflected firelight. It was nearly dark outside.

'I must go. Thank you for the tea.'

'I'm glad you came.' It was an understatement: she had been heaven-sent. He opened the door on a darkening wood. 'I'll come with you as far as the bridge.'

'Don't you lock the door?'

'Not while I'm here. Just think, if it had been locked today, we would never have met.'

In the wavering light of his oil lamp the privacy of their companionship continued until the light in the mill house gave warning of its end.

'I'll be back in the summer. Perhaps you'll come this way again.'

'Perhaps.'

He waited as she went quickly over the bridge, then turned back, walking under bare trees to the empty house. Now that she was gone it was worse than ever: he was so damned lonely. His feet on the flagged floor were loud enough for a whole platoon. The dark stairs mounted to rooms occupied by ghosts. He hated the place – and loved it as the only place where he had been happy: almost at home. He went into the cold kitchen, opened a tin of corned beef, cut slices of bread and like the old woman in the ballad, wished for company.

On her way to the Post Office next morning Lorna happened to be passing the station as the 10.15 for Donnerton approached. Unless he had gone by the 7 o'clock train, Julian must catch this one or wait until the afternoon. There were three or four people on the platform: two women, a workman with a bag of tools and a tall young man in dark city clothes and wearing a black hat. At first she didn't recognize him. Clothes make a difference, in this case a significant one.

PC Hawkes was walking his beat as she came out of the Post Office. She knew that he would make his usual joke.

'Never a button missing from my shirt, Miss Kent, since you taught our Maudie to sew them on.'

'Is there a clockmaker in Canterlow?' she asked when the buttons had been dealt with.

'No, there isn't, more's the pity. Not since old Mr Hood left for London. You'll find one or two in Gorsham though. There's Thomas and Ward. They see to the church clock.'

Relentlessly, because she didn't want to, she reminded herself of the case against Julian. He was there, at the Hammond house on the August evening of her first visit: he wore a black hat; he hated the local girl who had been the cause of ill-will between him and Digby, hated the very thought of her; and the local girl was Alice Hood, the clockmaker's daughter.

In 1916 his connection with her had probably been no more than a harmless flirtation with a pretty girl not yet sixteen. Afterwards she became the focus of his many frustrations, chiefly the guilt he felt for his shabby treatment of his cousin which he transferred to her: she was to blame. His hatred was irrational. He had come back and had been here at the time of her death.

Such was the case against him. One didn't have to believe it. She could not condemn him as she had recklessly condemned the unknown man with whom Alice Hood had been involved. Everything in his parentage, upbringing and experience had been against him, most of all the war. The harm it had done could not be summed up in figures of the dead: its ravages had destroyed thousands who were left alive. But why should an innocent girl for whom neither he nor Digby cared twopence be victimized? There was simply no connection.

Yet she had learned that things are not always what they seem. Presumably it was the same with people. Canterlow was a place where anything could happen, in a green glade screened by trees or by the dam or on the edge of a cliff by night or in an empty house. She remembered Roy's description of the Beam valley in spring: 'Fresh as a morning in Eden and as old as sin' and hoped with all her heart that if Julian had been involved in any but the most innocent way with Alice Hood, her sister would never hear of it.

# Chapter 19

Public opinion in Canterlow was slow to change and when it did the process was at first gradual: a matter of small adjustments whereby attention moved from one focus of interest to another.

Nora Webber was probably among the first to be aware of such a change, so slight that no one else had time to notice it. Certainly no one was better placed for knowing what went on in the town. The Webbers' house, No. 7 Victoria Terrace, had no front garden but the flagged square between the bay window and the iron railings was just big enough to accommodate a garden seat and on mild days Nora's reclining chair. For an enthusiastic snapper-up of trifles of news, the situation was ideal, so close to the pavement that no civil person could pass without a word.

Nora had been sitting there, bolstered by pillows and wrapped in a rug one Saturday morning when Roy Moxby came to the gate. It had taken him some time to find a reason for calling other than the obvious one of asking how she was. She must be sick and tired of people being kind. With all his faults he was a thoughtful young man. Always had been as his mother could testify – and still was.

'Sit down, Roy,' Nora indicated the seat. 'It's been a long time.'

She would scarcely have known him. It wasn't just that he had had his hair cut and his trousers pressed and had done something about his fingernails. The hint of flabbiness had gone; his eyes and complexion were clearer; he looked alert.

'I need your help. Do you mind? I thought you might know of someone who would take me in as a lodger.'

'So – you're moving out?' At last, she thought, and a jolly good thing too. 'Well now, let me think.' It didn't take long. 'Miss Craig in Church Lane has a room to let. Mr Dalton used to lodge there. He works for the Water Board but he's been transferred to Gorsham. He was very comfortable with Miss Craig. She's a dear old soul. Refined, you know. The Craigs used to live at Beam Hall. That would be in her grandfather's time. He lost all his money in the railway scandal. She has a little annuity from her father but hardly enough to live on.' There was nothing Nora didn't know about Miss Craig, a blameless woman with nothing to conceal.

'Do you think she'd take me?' Under Nora's candid gaze his fragile confidence wavered. 'I've turned over a new leaf, you know.'

'I can see that.' Bless his heart there wasn't a scrap of harm in him. 'Why don't you go there now this very minute and ask her? She charges 17/6 a week – a bit more if you want the sitting-room to yourself.'

'You think I should?' He was dazed by her apparent ease in dealing with what had seemed a problem. 'You've got everything at your fingertips, haven't you? Shall I call – to let you know the verdict?'

He was back in half an hour, flushed with success.

'I mentioned your name. Was that all right? Miss Craig didn't hesitate.' He was to have board and lodging, all found, washing done and the sitting-room to himself for a pound a week. 'I hadn't realized how pleasant it is in Church Lane. So quiet. Thank you from the bottom of my heart. You don't know what this means to me.'

'Drop in from time to time and let me know if all goes well.' She had a fair idea of what it meant to him to escape from

Councillor Garson to a room and a life of his own. He had gone to the gate. 'What time is it?'

'Twenty-eight minutes past ten.'

'It's nearly time. Sit down for a minute.'

'What's the mystery?'

'You'll see.'

And presently she came, walking so quietly that they did not hear her approach. They were not the only ones to wait and watch. Further down the street more than one doorknocker was being unnecessarily polished; at several windows curtains had been stealthily drawn back to allow a better view. But she did not turn her head – hatless, her shining hair falling smoothly to her waist, her skin as white as her blouse, her eyes fixed unwaveringly on the way ahead. But she did turn to look over the railings at No. 7 though without pausing in her steady walk.

'Good morning, Miss Webber – and Mr Moxby.'

'Good morning, Etta,' they said and when she had gone, they gazed at each other wide-eyed and for a moment mute.

'Every morning,' Nora said, 'and then again in the afternoon as regular as clockwork. She sits by the grave, then goes down to the dam and stays there – I don't know how long.'

'It's weird.'

'It's love.' There'll be no one to do that for me, she thought, when my time comes. They'll be sad. They won't forget me but I won't be remembered as Alice Hood is remembered.

Roy looked up the street. At one gate a little girl was waiting with a bunch of sweet peas. She held them out shyly. Etta took them, perhaps with a smile but without a moment's pause. On some days she was given more than one bunch to lay on Alice's grave.

She was becoming a feature of life in Canterlow. Not a day had she missed throughout a bitter winter. She was never seen with a companion. Her devotion had taken on in the eyes of observers a religious significance. Her quietness, her unfailing regularity, her loneliness, allied to her uncanny resemblance to her sister, seemed other-worldly and given time, would become legendary. Visitors were told of the phenomenon reverently and with pride and were hustled to windows at the appropriate times. The Hoods, forgotten for years and never much thought of except for the nine days' wonder of Alice's death, were reinstated as one of the town's oldest families. The buzz of talk was of a favourable kind.

'If ever a good girl was led astray, that girl was Alice Hood. . . . She put an end to herself. Some say suicide is a sin but it was her way of showing repentance. . . . She went to face her Maker and offer up her sin for His forgiveness. . . .' And more vindictively and dangerously, 'Seventeen years old and taken wicked advantage of.'

Somehow belated sympathy for Alice whom the world had so cruelly rejected was extended to include Etta, the living embodiment of her sister and – vaguely to minds given that way – a symbol of life after death. She was talked of a good deal, always in hushed tones and lowered voices. Her intriguing strangeness had a unifying effect. Even in the Ploughman's Inn the story of the Hoods had only to be mentioned to change the atmosphere. Arguments were silenced, heads shaken over a bad business, ears pricked for the latest driblet of news.

For reasons known only to himself and Lorna Kent the situation was of keener interest to Roy Moxby than to anyone else. His sitting room at Miss Craig's was no more than a stone's throw from the lych-gate through which Etta passed on her way to the grave and beyond, through the stile, to the dam. At weekends and during holidays he could see her on the outward journey; on weekdays he saw her coming back from her waterside meditation. At first it had been a distressing reminder of the boyhood dream he had been slow to outgrow and of the fearful experience in which it had ended. But gradually from sheer repetition the pangs of heart-sickness were assuaged: he could see Etta without writhing in shame for his cowardice in leaving Alice in the water, making no effort to revive her, however hopeless, and failing to report her death as any responsible human being would have done.

He began instead to feel a compensatory obligation to behave responsibly towards Etta. As far as he knew there was no one to keep an eye on her except Ushart and for some time now Ushart had been in no state to look after anybody. No man had ever been so broken down, presumably by the death of his wife. He had lost weight, lacked concentration and looked as if he had bad nights.

As for Etta, Roy had not forgotten Lorna's foreboding that she was up to no good. As far as he could tell there was no sign of evil intent in the poor girl's behaviour but he did wonder if she was in her right mind. Though he saw her often it was never close enough to see the look in her eyes, a sure test of the inner state, or to engage her in conversation, if indeed Etta ever conversed.

He mentioned his doubts about her sanity to Lorna whom he had not seen since his removal to Church Lane until he called one evening at the Webbers with a present for Nora and found the two of them together. His first impression as he joined Lorna on the garden seat was that she too looked less well than usual. What was happening to everybody?

There was no concealing the gift, a small folding table found in a second-hand shop in Gorsham.

'For your needlework. And it folds up quite small.' He demonstrated.

'Well, just look at that, Lorna. It'll be absolutely right next to the sofa. And you brought it all the way from Gorsham.' Nora's face shone with pleasure in the gift and even more in having been remembered.

'So you've branched out on your own,' Lorna said when every aspect of the table had been admired.

'I feel a different man and you must admit there was room for improvement.'

'Your mother?'

'She has taken it better than I thought, so long as I go for a meal from time to time. I believe she's relieved as a matter of fact.'

'One man is enough to look after,' Nora said and all three refrained from naming the man who was more than enough.

Roy and Lorna left together. He went with her as far as The Birches and found her less talkative than usual.

'Are you feeling quite well?'

'Yes, perfectly. Just rather tired.' She roused herself when he added, 'Do you think Etta Hood is unbalanced, mentally?' and gave him her full attention.

'So you've heard.'

He protested that he had heard nothing: the idea was entirely his own; he wondered if the girl needed help. They had reached The Birches where the garden was more commodious than the Webber's and a summerhouse offered seats and privacy. There had been developments at the schoolhouse, she told him. The suggestion of a friend that a compromise might be reached had been acted upon. Without consulting Mr Ushart who was not easy to talk to on the subject, her aunt had written a second time to Mrs McNab suggesting that she should come on a visit to 'talk things over' and adding that in the present circumstances she might prefer to stay at The Birches. Mrs McNab's prompt acceptance of the invitation seemed proof of her willingness to co-operate.

The two ladies had met for the first time and took to each other. Mrs McNab's appearance was reassuring. Her slightly rounded figure, pink cheeks, straightforward blue eyes and good plain tweeds, together with the fact that she had brought up two sons single-handed, both now doing well in the Civil Service, so perfectly fitted her for the position of housekeeper and foster-mother that, as Aunt Mabel said, 'The children of royalty could not be better served.' They both felt that the tiresome difficulty need never have arisen and that Mrs McNab should be welcomed back with a fanfare of trumpets.

The relationship between the three had been sufficiently comfortable for Lorna to ask: 'I wonder – why do you feel that you can't live in the same house as Etta Hood?'

'I could have and I intended to, for the children's sake,' Mrs McNab's reply had been tearful, 'and for their mother's. Blood is thicker than water and Madeline was my second cousin on the Templeton side. But when I heard more about the girl's condition' – she dabbed her eyes and shook her head – 'I know she can't help it but I couldn't be expected to deal with that sort of thing.'

'What sort of thing?' Aunt Mabel asked in some alarm. 'What can't she help?'

'Being out of her mind. It isn't the poor girl's fault but with insanity in the house there's no knowing what might happen. One hears of such terrible things.'

'Dear me! I had no idea. Mr Ushart did mention that she had what he called morbid tendencies, whatever that means.'

Far from being solved, the problem was assuming a more sinister colouring.

'I don't think it's true,' Lorna said. 'Etta is certainly strange but she has never shown signs of violence or done or said anything that could be called – crazy.' She hesitated, remembering that the thought had crossed her mind the first time she saw Etta. 'You said you heard that she was out of her mind, Mrs McNab. Who told you?'

'Why who else but Mr Ushart. . . .'

'I suppose he's in a position to know,' Roy said when Lorna had given him the gist of the conversation. 'Presumably he also knows that there is no threat to the children. I wonder how he can be sure of that.'

'Of course he must be sure. He told both Tilly and Mrs McNab that Etta might behave strangely and say things that couldn't possibly be true but they were to pay no attention.'

'What sort of things?'

Pondering on the remarkably few statements she had heard Etta make, Lorna could not recall any wildness in them. They had sometimes seemed wrung from the heart and were never casual or superficial, always true. Could Etta's extraordinary singleness of mind be a sign of insanity?

'In any case,' she said, 'there is no need to worry about Paul and Amy for the time being. Mrs McNab has taken them back with her to Scotland.'

'The logical thing for him to do would be to marry Mrs McNab. If she'll have him.'

When he had gone, Lorna leaned back wearily, her head on the white slats of the summerhouse. His last remark had cut her to the quick. Aunt Mabel had made a similar one, several times. It would be a sensible solution. The children had been overjoyed to see Auntie McNab. They had rushed into her arms to be hugged and held as they had not been for months and had left for Scotland, so far as she knew, without a tear.

How lonely he must be! He needed a wife, one who would love and understand him and had known him in happier days. She remembered him as he had been when they first met: self-confident, master of himself as well as of his small domain. She thought of the sudden smile, the light of humour in his eyes, his vivid face, the varied tones of his voice – soft and low, stern and commanding – and she was ashamed. He had asked her to marry him. He wanted her, not Mrs McNab. 'I need you,' he had said, a break in his voice, 'more than anything in the world.' She had drawn away from him like a gawky schoolgirl at the very moment of his deepest need.

She had chosen to be fastidious because his kiss had seemed

impersonal; because he had seemed preoccupied; because she had preferred to dream of the rapture of love rather than face its reality and accept its imperfections. He had promised to wait; had begged her not to make him wait too long. He would ask her again. Surely she must accept: it was the right thing to do. Had not Madeline told her so?

To remember Madeline was to feel again like a chilling breeze the misgiving that had troubled her: a foreshadowing, as if gazing at smooth untroubled waters, one thought with appre-hension of what lay beneath. She sat on in the twilight, learning what Madeline had learned before her. The fulfilment of one's dearest wish is granted on one condition: it must be paid for.

It occurred to her that she might write to Adam, setting down clearly the reasons for her hesitation. This felt so much like taking a positive step that she failed to recognize it as merely a prolonging of uncertainty, and went at once to her room, sat down at her bureau, found notepaper and dipped her pen in ink with something like a wordless prayer that she would, if not now then soon, do the right thing; or at least be shown what was the right thing to do.

The bureau had been Aunt Belle's. Apart from making space for her own letters from her father and friends, she had left its arrangements unchanged: in the miniature drawers a medley of pen-nibs, wax-ends and pen-holders; in the slots, débris left by the owner – several letters, funeral and wedding cards, receipted bills. . . .

*Dear Adam. . . .*

Minutes passed. Her eyes strayed at last from the blank page. Still mentally forming her first sentence, she pulled out one of the drawers, shut it, put down her pen, tightened the screw on the handle of her blotter, tidied the letters written to Aunt Belle. She had not read them: one didn't read other people's letters.

One of them in a square grey envelope jutted out of the slot. The stamp was unfamiliar: Mr Shackleton would have recognized it of course. It was addressed to Miss Featherstone and bore a printed label: *Returned to Sender.* Inside was another envelope, unopened and addressed to Miss E. Stowe at a town in Ottawa. The fly-by-night Stowes must have taken flight once more.

It seemed an intrusion to open the letter but to read it would be like hearing Aunt Belle's voice, speaking from that lost world at the turn of the century when the death of the old Queen ushered in the golden Edwardian age: a time of croquet lawns and carriages, ladies' maids and man-servants, before the war swept most of them away.

*Dearest Evelyn,*
*It is so long since I heard from you that I have been quite worried. . . .*

In those days Belle had not yet acquired the stately tone she was to feel appropriate for letter writing in her maturer years. Presumably she took to reading novels at a later date, for consolation perhaps. This was a simple heart-to-heart appeal for news of a dear friend whom it had never reached.

*You asked me to tell you about my own affairs. There is nothing new since I last wrote. . . .*

The letter was dated August, 1905. Sifting through the wedding cards, Lorna found the one that mattered. Morton Liffey and Dora Forgill had been married in 1898.

*My feelings will never change and I do not believe he has changed any more than I have. We are never alone together for more than a minute or two but I have seemed to see a sadness in his eyes, probably because I wanted to. I happened to ask the other day if he was disappointed that the Australian order was cancelled. He confessed*

182

*that he was. 'You understand, Belle,' he said. 'We've learned that
life is full of regrets – and wrong decisions, haven't we?' I felt sure
that he wasn't thinking about the Australian order. You are the only
person in the world I have confided in except Aggie. There's no
deceiving her.*

*We had our usual trip to the seaside yesterday. The children loved
the beach and especially the donkey rides, although Rita was sick.
We got her off the swing-boat in time but I'm afraid the state of her
dress cast a cloud. Cedric kept an eye on the younger ones. Lorna
looked very sweet in white with blue ribbons and insisted on keeping
her mittens on all day. I do miss hearing from you. . . .*

Belle had not bothered to reread her own letter nor had she
brought herself to the finality of destroying it, though the official
grey envelope with its peremptory label banished any hope she
might have had of hearing from Evelyn again. Dear Aunt Belle!
Somehow, as Aggie said, she had missed the boat and stayed
ashore among the donkeys and swing-boats and other people's
children. A woman who never married must inevitably slip into
the background, waiting to lend a helpful hand with other
people's families, especially the children, and to grow fond of
them. Young Kents, for instance, or Liffeys. Or Usharts?

Lorna put the card back with the others, a permanent
reminder of how easy it was to let happiness slip through one's
fingers, and thought of Aunt Belle as a guest, dry-eyed and
stoical, at Morton's wedding; thought of her going home afterwards to spend the rest of her life alone. She too had loved a
married man. If Dora had died. . . ? Surely, almost certainly, Belle
would have married Morton.

There was no need to write to Adam, nor was it necessary to
tear her sheet of notepaper into such very small shreds when
there were only two words to conceal. It took a little time: a
dreamlike occupation of which she was barely conscious,
possessed as she was by the clear knowledge of what she must do.

Her prayer had been answered. The letter had reminded her of all that she would gain in marrying him and all that marriage would save her from – the life-long loneliness of a single woman. It was wrong to have kept him waiting, wrong to have thought of writing. She had simply to tell him, to speak the one simple word he wanted to hear.

The room darkened round her. She went to bed without lighting the lamp. . . .

In Miss Craig's sitting-room Roy Moxby also sat alone – to his intense satisfaction – as twilight fell. He too was in a reflective mood. His reverie, based on the same material as Lorna's, took a different form. It was more impartial though not completely so: his attitude to the leading actor in the drama at the schoolhouse had been too much fraught with discomfort to leave him entirely unprejudiced.

What kind of man would take into his home a former pupil whom he believed to be mentally unbalanced and therefore unpredictable when by so doing he must lose the ideal foster-mother or better still stepmother for his children – and let them go too? As Lorna had suspected it was impossible to share the same roof or even the same table with Councillor Garson without hearing a good deal that should have been privy to members of the eleven committees on which he so heavily sat. The advice given to Ushart after the unofficial meeting at The Birches had been repeated at the Garson dinner table.

'The man'll have to marry if he expects me to help him to the school at Maywick when old Birkett passes on.'

Nevertheless the man had let the most suitable wife slip through his fingers.

At this point Roy's train of thought took another direction. It would be a long time before he ceased to gloat over the manner in which he had left the Garson home. Having embraced his mother and shaken hands with his stepfather, he had produced from his pocket a small object retrieved from the Hammond house by way of the cellar door.

'I believe this is yours.' He had achieved what he felt to be a meaningful leer. 'You should be careful where you take your shirt off, you know.' The satisfaction of seeing a purple flush suffuse those parts of the Councillor's face left uncovered by his moustache repaid many small humiliations.

His thought turned to Etta Hood. He had been moved by her daily pilgrimages. Again he had difficulty in taking an impartial view: she was so like the girl he had idolized as to be inseparable from his memory of Alice. He went to the window. A few minutes later she appeared at the lych-gate like a ghost in the dusk: in summer she sometimes dressed entirely in white. Was her unwavering dedication to her sister's memory a sign of insanity or of considerable powers of self-discipline concentrated on a single purpose? The ultra-sanity of genius? The proposition intrigued him. Ushart had predicted that her behaviour might be strange. It was. He had also predicted that she might say things that couldn't possibly be true. What sort of things?

He lit his lamp and settled in his armchair with a volume of Browning's poems, determined at last to get down to the Epistle of Karshish to Abib and if possible discover what it actually meant. Miss Craig tapped and entered, bearing his bedtime hot drink.

'Goodnight and God bless you, Mr Moxby,' she said.

'Thank you and you too, Miss Craig.'

Night darkened the uncurtained window. An owl glided from the belfry to the nearest elm. Its eerie cry roused him from his book. He looked round the lamp-lit room – his own – and went on reading, a happy man. He had never dreamed that life could be so interesting.

# Chapter 20

'It's from Mrs McNab.' Aunt Mabel passed the letter to Lorna at the breakfast table. 'The children have settled very well.'

Mrs McNab wrote apologetically. There had been so little time for the packing that one or two things had been forgotten. Paul had just discovered that one of his soldiers was missing. She had never known him so upset. He thought Tilly might be able to find it. She wondered if their heavier boots could also be sent on.

'It's one thing to send a toy soldier and quite another to parcel up two pairs of boots, even children's. She'll be lucky if they haven't grown out of them since last winter. Still, she's doing her best, I will say that for her. Gladys can go for the things when she's done the dishes.'

'No. I'll go.' Lorna's words positively rang in her own ears. She had not meant to sound so forceful. They were the words of a person who had screwed her courage to the sticking place. Her face reflected in the sideboard mirror was pale and tense.

'Perhaps you'd better.' Aunt Mabel had not noticed. 'If the soldier has to be hunted for it will take time and Gladys has Aggie's room to turn out.'

It would be best, obviously, to postpone one's visit to the schoolhouse until late afternoon when Adam was most likely to be at home. The decision brought a faint, irrational sense of relief. Meanwhile there was the lesser problem of finding a birthday present for Faith, no easy task. It must be something small, neither frivolous nor expensive – no perfume or pretti-ness; Faith would not approve. A simple token of friendship and good wishes – Faith had used those very words on a previ-ous occasion – was all that was required. Something cheap and plain yet of a quality worthy of Faith. The only safe thing was a book.

Lorna spent the morning in Gorsham in an increasingly desperate search. There was nothing in either of the bookshops that she could be sure Faith would like and did not already possess. Her train would leave in ten minutes. Passing through the market-place on her way to the station by a side street, she caught sight of a third bookshop, its narrow frontage almost hidden by the display of walking-sticks and besoms outside the shop next door.

It was below ground level; the stairs were unlit. Stepping down into its murky darkness was to have a significance she could not have foreseen. It was there that she found the right book: an exact replica of one she had herself been given and would never part with: a slim little volume bound in red, a span in length, three inches wide and light as a feather. She pictured Faith groping for it in her capacious handbag and snatching a few minutes of escape from tram or train, from Brandon or Hookgate, from workhouse, hospital or soup kitchen.

'Just the one, ma'am?' The proprietor paused before wrap-ping it up.

'You have others?'

'The whole edition. Six volumes. They came in yesterday. A house clearance. The gentleman had died. He was a good customer. I'm going to miss him.'

'I'll take all of them.'

'I'm pleased to hear it and so would he be. They're meant to be kept together – and every one of them intact. Not a page missing or even loose.'

The complete works of Shakespeare in the Arden Pocket Edition! She would keep all but the first volume and have the whole edition complete except for the double page Adam had torn out. She had given up trying to find the gap but it would be easier to identify with the help of an identical volume than with Uncle Arthur's massive *Complete Works*. Unfortunately it would take time and the present must be posted tomorrow.

At The Birches lunch was almost ready. She ran upstairs, undid the parcel, tumbled the books out on the bed, found the one intended for Faith, flicked through the pages to check that none was damaged – and found an illustration she had never seen before.

Not only had she found it at once, amazingly, miraculously, and in the nick of time – she also understood at once why he had torn it out. It was a revelation. Her heart warmed to him as never before, not in quite this way. Indeed it was from his own warmth of heart that he had acted that day before holding out the book, his face hidden from her in a shimmer of sunlight. Had he even then felt that her sympathies were in accord with his own, that their feelings were attuned?

She gazed at the picture with something like awe. It was Millais' *The Death of Ophelia*. She had not known that such a picture existed; even now she was seeing it only in monochrome, its melancholy unrelieved by colour: the fantastic garlands of crowflowers, nettles, daisies and long purples subdued to varying shades of grey; the weeping brook black; the face of the drowned girl uncannily pale.

Local affairs had played no part in her conversations with Adam: they had talked of other things. The Hood tragedy had never been mentioned: there had been no occasion to speak of it. Consequently she had given no thought to the effect it must have had on him – the suicide of one of his pupils – with her sister then still in his school. Yet from the very first she had felt his sensitivity, had seemed to recognize in him depths of nature that made him different from other men. But now it was the thought of his compassion that moved her. What clearer proof could there be than his protective attitude towards Etta? It was an act of pure Christian charity to take her in, knowing that the gossip about her mental state would discourage everyone else from giving her a home or even offering shelter.

All this she felt – and more. She had again, quite by chance, been reminded of Alice Hood. The affinity between them, felt from the beginning, dismissed as merely fanciful and not to be indulged, was no illusion. This time it had not taken the form of a warning. It had been a signal reminding her of the true nature of the man she loved, pointing out the direction she should take. She looked again at the picture and was over-whelmed by pity for the drowned girl – as Adam had been. She was seeing him now as the man he really was, as she had always felt him to be. She closed the book, no longer hesitant or afraid.

He saw her waiting in the garden when school was dismissed. Miss Prior and Miss Ellwood also saw her and waved as they crossed the yard.

'Are you thinking what I'm thinking?' Miss Ellwood asked.

'Probably,' Miss Prior replied.

The same thought inspired the headmaster to glance in the cloakroom mirror and to feel despondent at the sight of his haggard face, brow furrowed, cheeks sunken. He ran a comb though his hair. This last vile year had aged him: it had been of a kind to age any man. His health had suffered and now the uncertainty as to why Lorna had come, deliberately, when for months they had not been alone together, kept him hesitant at the door before going to meet her. He had no clue as to what she had come to tell him: whether to put him out of his misery with a definite refusal or to safeguard his future by an acceptance. He had spirit enough left to feel a kind of rage that he should be dependent on her answer: indeed spurts of anger, feverish and unprovoked, had troubled him increasingly during the past few weeks.

She had come down the path to meet him.

'I've been wanting to see you, Adam.'

'A very welcome sight.'

She looked charming in a pale summer dress and wide-brimmed hat. He took out a pocket-knife and cut a rose. Her hand trembled as she took it and looked down into its crimson heart. Changed though he was, he had not lost the art of transforming the commonplace with a touch of elegance. In her eyes he had always been a romantic figure. She smiled, feeling more at ease, reminding herself that he loved her and wanted her more than any other woman in the world. Had he not said so?

'You find me changed?' The unexpected question touched her.

'You do look tired, Adam. I don't know whether you have changed in any other way.'

'Not in loving you, my dearest. And you?'

'I have loved you for a long time. Since the beginning.' It seemed the only significant span of time in her life as though she had not really existed before they met. To be with him again was to regret the months she had wasted in trying to make up her mind. It had been for them both a sentence of imprisonment when there had been no offence.

'You have kept me waiting a long time. I had almost given up hope. If I ask you again now – will you marry me?' He took her hand and kissed it.

'You've been patient. I should not have left you as I did but I felt then that it was too soon.' Nor had there been the same need to rescue him: a curious word to use when she had always looked up to him as in every way her superior. She remembered as if it had happened in a previous existence that as a girl she had not aspired to anything more than to be useful. It might still be a consolation to think of herself in that way, though she might have wondered why at such a poignant moment consolation should be needed; or why she should be glad that these strangely muted exchanges were taking place here in the garden where he could do no more than kiss her hand a second time, with a quick glance towards the house though they were well out of sight of both it and the lane.

There was no need now to conceal their engagement: it would soon be a year since Madeline died; yet almost in the same breath they both found reasons for postponing the announcement.

'Are you prepared for the talk there will be? It will be well intentioned I'm sure, but people do like to have something to talk about.'

'I wouldn't like it at all.' It was the one thing she could be sure of though there was no reason why the people she cared about should not be pleased. They should be delighted, she thought, as they sprang into line to congratulate her: Aunt Mabel, Aggie, Faith, Nora, Roy, her father, the Liffeys. And Cedric. 'Perhaps we should wait the full year,' she said.

'So long as I'm sure of you, my love.'

'You've been through so much. It's important for you to live quietly for a while.'

Then in a few weeks, their number undefined, they would be quietly married; she would slip into the schoolhouse and begin to devote her life to caring for him. Well-cooked meals, a comfortable fireside and his children at home again would restore his health and peace of mind. Instinctively she banished the green sofa and moved the table to the middle of the room. Her mind strayed to the long dim bedroom: the drawers and wardrobe full of Madeline's clothes; the big brass bed with Madeline in it.

She knew that she was deceiving herself. Her smug picture of cosy domestic bliss was out of keeping with his ravaged looks and subdued manner. Peace of mind could not be restored by good housekeeping and a faithful, useful wife; nor could grief for Madeline fully account for its loss. She was feeling as before that his thoughts were elsewhere. He was in conflict as if prey to some hidden canker more virulent than grief. 'Marry him – and soon,' Madeline had urged. 'You're the kind of girl men marry for the right reasons. . . . A man can be misled by inclinations you know nothing of. . . .'

Her urgency had been that of a sick woman for whom time was running out. To suggest that Adam could be misled had been no more than a touch of delirium.

'And Etta?' she now asked.

'Etta? She will go, of course. As a matter of fact we may not be in Canterlow for long after we are married.'

'You may go to another school?'

'It's possible. I hope to and then we can begin a new life together.'

She left by the school gate instead of going back to the house. Her eyes as she faced him to say goodbye were less serene than they had been on the day when they first met. Nothing, he had felt then, had happened to disturb her tranquillity: it was all still to come – the harrowing pain of love, the destructive power of passion. She still had much to learn. Still, she had given him what he wanted – and would give him much more. . . .

Lorna had Abbot's Lane to herself. It was here that the spell had fallen upon her on that first day. There had been a hint of spring in the air. She had heard children's voices singing and had responded with delight to the harmony of sky, trees and stone-tiled school in its sheltered hollow. It had been like stepping out of time into a region with all the charm of the material world and none of its bewildering changes.

Tilly was waiting for her at the corner where the lane joined the street.

'You forgot these, miss.' She held out a brown paper parcel.

'I'm sorry, Tilly. It was stupid of me.'

'I found the boots easy enough but I haven't been able to lay hands on the soldier. There's plenty of places I could look if I had the time. I know how Paul feels about his soldiers. He played with them for hours.'

'Shall I come one morning and help to look for it?'

'If you would, miss. It would be like old times to see you about the place again.'

Aggie was back in her room and had gone to bed.

'I'm in the lap of luxury here,' she said when Lorna came to say goodnight. 'I'll never forget what you and Mrs Hobcroft have done for me, and Mr Cedric bringing me in his motor car, not to my dying day. But you'll not have to put up with me much longer. It's about time I got back into harness.'

Her one regret was that for the past weeks Lorna had not seemed herself. She had a strained look and not much to say. Aggie had more than once been on the point of asking if anything was wrong but had held her tongue, hoping to be confided in as had sometimes happened in the past. Mrs Hobcroft was all very well and kinder than she had expected, but she hadn't lived with Lorna day in and day out since she was a baby and didn't know her ins and outs as she herself did.

'You'll happen to be taking a trip to Donnerton before long,' she ventured. 'You always enjoy the shops and taking a walk on the moor.' With Mr Cedric, she felt like saying. 'Then there'll be the Cutlers' Ball again. . . .' What was the girl thinking about to make her seem a hundred miles away?

'One of these days we'll have a really good talk,' Lorna said, 'the way we used to.'

It would be a relief to confide in Aggie and find words for the nameless apprehension that hung about her at the very time when she should have been happier than ever before. To feel a wave of homesickness for the old days in Donnerton was sheer perversity when she had just turned her back on it for good.

# Chapter 21

'So you think she might really' – Nora paused before adding in a lower, more thrilling tone – 'marry him?'

'Well, there she was in the garden waiting for him,' Miss Ellwood said.

'And looking a picture.' Miss Prior's tribute was affectionate but tinged with something like regret as Nora was quick to notice.

'It would be a good thing, wouldn't it?'

'He'd be a lucky man.'

Their verdict was unanimous though no specific reason emerged for believing that the luck was not on Lorna's side. But as the warm weather continued and Nora spent a good deal of time in the little paved area between the bay window and the iron railings at No. 7, it soon became common knowledge that 'something was going on' between the headmaster and Mrs Hobcroft's niece; and an interested observer might have noticed that praise of Mr Ushart who had always been so highly regarded was becoming lukewarm.

For one thing he looked different. He appeared to have shrunk physically as well as in public esteem. He even looked a little untidy and his manner was sometimes morose. In school his eye was less keen for detail: things were overlooked that should have been pounced on. There had even been a Friday – Nora could scarcely believe her ears when Miss Ellwood told her – when the final checking of the registers for the week had been left to Mr Shackleton.

'And he's never stopped boasting about it.' Miss Prior would not herself have mentioned so deplorable a lapse on Mr Ushart's part. All the same she had seen it as very grave. If the headmaster could not attend to the registers, she should have been the one to deputize, not a comparative newcomer with his head full of stamps. It worried her that Mr Ushart should have made so flagrant an error of judgement. It had been a downward step.

Public opinion had been favourable when he employed Etta Hood at the schoolhouse but when it was rumoured that he had raised doubts about Etta's sanity, voices were raised in protest. By that time Etta had come to be regarded as an asset to the town: a lonely girl with only one thought in her mind – to do right by her dead sister. If that was a sign of insanity it was a pity more people didn't take leave of their senses, especially educated people who ought to know better.

There could be little doubt as to the source of that particular rumour. Anxious, overworked and disregarded, Tilly became briefly a person worth talking to. The questions people asked confused her. She didn't know what to say except to deny anything she had already said. Nevertheless no one else could have let it be known that 'Mrs Ushart couldn't bear him to come near her', a statement much quoted with the significant addition, 'Poor lady'.

At The Birches the first person to hear what was being said about Miss Lorna and Mr Ushart was Gladys. It was not her business to tell Mrs Hobcroft, but it was only human to mention it to Aggie one evening when she took up her bedtime drink and sat by her bed for a few minutes as she often did.

'There can't be anything in it,' Aggie said. 'Lorna would have told me. An important thing like that? Of course she would.

Don't you say a word about it, Gladys. If it's true I want to hear it from her own lips.' What she meant was that she did not want to hear it from Mrs Hobcroft's.

'They're saying he hasn't wasted much time.'

'Common people will say anything.'

But Aggie's disdain was unconvincing. She was hurt that Lorna had not told her and hardly slept a wink that night. That Lorna should be the subject of any kind of talk was bad enough, but if she was going to be married it should be arranged properly and openly and not in a hole and corner fashion; and, most importantly, it must be to the right man. If the rumour was true, someone else besides herself was going to be disappointed. In the normal course of events the gossip would have speedily reached Mrs Hobcroft's ears but she had been more than usually busy at home with no time for paying calls or receiving visitors. Aggie would soon be well enough to go home. Cedric would come and fetch her, bringing his mother who would stay for a week. This entailed a second spring-cleaning and a complete overhaul of the larder and stock cupboard. To the outside world Aunt Mabel was for the time being blind and deaf.

Waiting in a garden and looking like a picture is no guarantee of a forthcoming marriage. There could scarcely be a more flimsy foundation for gossip. But there was nothing flimsy about Councillor Garson.

'I saw Ushart last night,' he told his wife as he waited for his dinner. 'Are you listening?'

'Yes, yes.' She was always nervous when he sat at table while she was dishing up. 'I'm listening.' She brought the platter of roast lamb, piping hot, and remained standing while he carved. It had been a worry trying to keep a separate serving of potatoes and garden peas warm for Roy, who would come later when he was sure his stepfather would have finished.

'I'll pop this back on the oven top to keep hot.' She snatched away the platter.

'Sit down, woman, and pass the mint sauce. He's seen sense at last. He's going to get married.'

'It's soon, isn't it? After Mrs Ushart, I mean.'

'It's just in time if you ask me. Old Birkett at Maywick isn't going to last much longer from all I hear. I've told Ushart time and again that he has no chance of that promotion without a wife or the promise of one. I'll have more gravy.'

'Did he say who?'

'A friend of yours. Miss Kent. The right sort for him. Prim and particular.'

Mrs Garson poured out gravy with her mind on Roy. She wondered what he would think of the news. She had not long to wait. He arrived a few minutes after his stepfather had gone upstairs to take off his collar, tie and jacket and have forty winks before going off to Gorsham to a meeting in County Hall.

'Roast lamb? It isn't Sunday.'

'He likes a good dinner when he's going to Gorsham. It's usually too late for anything hot by the time he gets back.' She watched Roy as he ate. He looked well and handsome as he used to do. The cloud had lifted. She was sure Miss Kent had helped in some way and dreaded passing on the news.

'You're very quiet, mother.'

'A few more potatoes?'

But he had eaten well and would be off before she had found the best way of putting it. He thought a lot of Miss Kent. If he had hopes in that direction, the disappointment might put him back on the wrong road again. Perhaps after all she need not be the one to tell him, not just yet. On the other hand he ought to be prepared in case someone else blurted it out.

Words were not easy to find. As she pondered how to begin, it came to her in a flash that the best way would be to repeat exactly what Mr Garson had said, so far as she could remember. That would remove the responsibility to a higher authority. It would be like something in the newspaper that nobody could do anything about.

'Mr Garson saw Mr Ushart last night,' she began. 'He has come to his senses at last.'

'Not Mr Garson?' There was no hope of that.

'No. Mr Ushart.'

'What about?' Roy was instantly alert.

'Getting married and just in time.' She had already lost the thread. 'No, no. Nothing like that. Not when it's Miss Kent he's going to marry.'

Her worst fears were being confirmed before her very eyes. Her son's face had darkened, whether with anger or disappointment she could not tell. She had done the wrong thing this time and no mistake.

'Why *did* you say "just in time"?'

'Because that's what Mr Garson said. It was to do with Mr Birkett over at Maywick. He isn't going to last much longer, poor man. Mr Garson had told Mr Ushart time and again' – it was all coming back to her – 'that he can't be promoted without a wife.'

Roy rose from his chair so abruptly that it fell to the floor with a crash.

'Ssh!' His mother looked nervously at the ceiling. 'You'll wake him.'

But Roy was already at the door. He remembered to thank her for a good dinner and left.

If the news had come from Ushart himself it must be true. They must be in love. No one could help loving Lorna and presumably she loved Ushart. His mother had been mistaken: he had never even dreamed of marrying Lorna; she was far too good for him and miles beyond his reach. But he cared for her as a friend whose sympathy had restored his confidence in himself. There was no one whose friendship he valued more. His first reaction had been one of surprise. It was soon followed by his discovery that there were aspects of the affair that he disliked. Even allowing for the brutish insensitivity of his stepfather in speaking of Lorna as a pawn in some squalid manoeuvre – 'He can't be promoted without a wife' – the timing of Ushart's proposal had presumably been no coincidence. Though she couldn't possibly know it, she was being used.

From daily contact with Ushart he was aware of his deterioration. In his present state the man was unfit for promotion with or without a wife. Roy could not condemn him: he himself had been unfit for employment of any kind and had been rescued just in time. The death of his wife and frustrated ambition might cause a man to go to pieces and snatch at any means of saving himself from ruin. That was hardly the way to describe the winning of such a prize as Lorna, nor had Ushart's demeanour in recent months been that of a lover, happy and successful in his wooing. What was the matter with him?

In his sanctum in Church Lane he gave his mind to the problem, exercising with some enjoyment the powers of thought claimed for him by his mother and inherited presumably from his father. His analysis of the headmaster's character and behaviour brought him once more to the unaccountable presence of Etta Hood at the schoolhouse. Affording protection to a former pupil with morbid tendencies was surely praiseworthy: it was the action of a Good Samaritan but one unlikely to bring him peace of mind. He had let it be known that she might make wild and irresponsible statements. He must have heard some of them. What had she said, what might she say that was not to be believed?

The summer holiday was little more than half over. With an agreeable sense of leisure Roy went for a walk, then settled down in the long light evening to disentangle the contorted sentences of Karshish's letter to Abib; and – not for the first time when so employed – fell asleep, to wake with a start as the brown volume slid from his knee to the floor.

Yawning, he picked it up and with an effort of will turned the
pages back to the epistle of Karshish the physician on the raising
of the dead.

# Chapter 22

Sometimes Etta chose the south side of the dam where she could look across the water to the hilly pasture and the belt of trees on the ridge. In winter, chimneys could be seen between their bare branches. She had never seen the house. It did not interest her. On the south side the sheltering hill was steeper. Trees came closer to the water. It was boggy underfoot. Usually she stayed on the other south-facing side, walking up and down or sitting in one of her favourite nooks. Seasons passed her by. Coltsfoot and celandine, wood anemones and violets bloomed and withered without her noticing them. Elder flowers and may blossom draped the hedges and shed their florets. She trod on fallen petals without distinguishing them from the dust. Taller flowers, more likely to last on Alice's grave sometimes caught her eye but willow-herb, angelica and meadow-sweet were a poor substitute for the marvellous bouquet Miss Kent had given her.

'I'll give them to you and you can give them to Alice,' she had said.

The cuckoo came and went. Swallows would soon be gathering in flocks and bullfinches pecking at the berries of honeysuckle now scentless. There was movement everywhere. Birds had mated and raised their broods. The secret underwater world seethed with life. On its surface green weeds writhed and twisted above myriads of organisms. Dragonflies hovered. Only Etta sat still, thinking of Alice.

Her trouble was that she did not know the right place and had no means of finding out except through her own feelings. There were certain places where she felt the tremor of discovery. It was here? Her last footprints must have been here between the reeds. There were moments when the ache of longing became so intense that, gazing across the water, she almost saw Alice rise from it. With all the force of her heart and mind, all the hunger of starvation, she willed her to appear, to come back, to be alive again. Sometimes it was when the reflection of leaves on the other side was pierced by the shimmer of sunlight. Sometimes when morning mist still hung over the water or when a breeze sighed among the reeds, the sense of expectation was suddenly so acute, so bitterly misleading that she laid her head on her knees and cried.

Sitting with her back against a tree trunk or in the lee of the low wall separating meadow from pasture, she would remember the time before it happened. From the beginning Alice had been there to teach her how to dress herself, do her hair and wash from head to foot. Alice had taught her that some things were rude and should not be said or done. From Alice she learned what older girls talked about. When she went to bed she used to stay awake deliberately until Alice came upstairs and as she undressed, told her whom she had seen and what they had said, then slipped into her long nightdress and climbed into her half of the bed. The last thing she heard at night was Alice's quiet breath. Waking in the morning, she could turn her head and see Alice's head on her white pillow, her long braids of hair lying on the counterpane.

The nightdresses Etta wore then had been Alice's when she was younger. She was still wearing the same ones Alice had made for herself and had left behind. Now that she was as old as Alice had been, she could look at her hand and see a replica of Alice's and hear in her own voice an echo of her sister's.

One afternoon she was sitting on the grass with nothing

between her and the dam but the narrow path close to the water's edge when she heard someone coming down the hill behind her and turning, saw that it was Mr Moxby. He was wearing a jersey and knickerbockers with a canvas bag slung over his shoulder and was carrying a fishing rod. In the fresh air he seemed different and younger than the person he had been in school.

'I hope I didn't startle you.' He had deliberately come from behind. If she had seen him coming she would very likely have gone away. 'Do you mind if I join you? It's been a long walk to Fordham and back.' He unslung his bag, laid down his rod and sat down some little distance from her. 'Perhaps you don't feel like talking. No? Then I won't disturb you. Only there's no one else I can talk to about Alice.'

It was a risk he had resolved to take. The effect was immediate. If a statue had drawn breath and warmed into life the change could not have been more remarkable. No one had ever said that; no one had wanted to talk to her about Alice. Since there was nothing else in the world to talk about, she had been as if stricken dumb. Now in an instant her tongue had loosened; her eyes glowed; a faint colour stained her cheeks.

'She came here,' she said.

'I know. Do you sometimes feel that she is still here?'

'Yes – and presently – I want to find the place where I'll feel closest to her.' As it happened she was not far from the spot where he had seen Alice for the last time but he foresaw the danger in her search for physical closeness. The day might come when she would take the final step in following Alice. 'I keep looking.'

'Have you tried looking up?'

She raised her eyes. Between soft white clouds stretched endless vistas of summer blue. The sky surprised her. It was beautiful, immense and gentle.

'I'm sorry I frightened you that day in the churchyard, sir.'

'It wasn't your fault. You needn't call me "sir" now. We're just two people who loved Alice. She was a little girl when I first noticed her and she seemed more beautiful every time I saw her.' It occurred to him that she, like Lorna, might think that he had been Alice's lover. 'But I never even spoke to her.'

'Alice would have told me if you had. She told me everything.'

'Everything?'

'Yes.' She looked up again at the immense stretch of blue beyond billowing white clouds and when she rested her eyes on the familiar dam, darkened on the far side by trees, it seemed small, imprisoned in the earth.

'Do you ever feel like going back to London?'

Reminded of it, she tried to think about London. It was a name: she could not picture it. In the intensity of her need to come back to Canterlow she had been immune to impressions of other places. A blur of streets, the boarding house, a succession of unfamiliar faces had formed no more than a background against which she moved as if walking in her sleep until she could be free to go home to Alice.

'No,' she said.

He sensed in her a concentration of feeling she would never be able to express in words and wondered if it would find expression in other ways. Lorna had been fairly sure that it would. He had no wish to speculate on what form they would take. The sudden release of emotion so tightly coiled might be alarming. Lorna had assumed that Etta was bent on revenge.

He watched her as she gazed across the water, a slight ignorant girl. 'Revenge' was too bold and savage a term for anything she might do even if her victim could be found. Yet the way of life she had adopted was a demonstration of extraordinary inner strength. She would go her own way, as indifferent to laws human and divine as she had been to bitter weather and gaping neighbours.

His interest in her had been genuine but there had been in it an element of self-interest too. Since the confidential talk with Lorna among the lime kilns he had felt some relief from the shame of his unmanly behaviour when he found Alice's body; but he was still haunted by guilt. To see Etta in the setting where he had last seen her sister was in some way a test. He had seen her there several times. At first it was like seeing Alice but today for the first time Alice had withdrawn. She had never possessed – certainly not for him – Etta's amazing strength. He had thought of Alice as gentle because she looked gentle. Etta looked exactly like her but her individuality, as Lorna said, was unique. In talking to Etta he had ceased to think of Alice.

'What are your plans now that you've come back?' He spoke heartily as to any young person on the threshold of life, but with a sense of casting caution to the winds. She was no longer looking at the sky but at him. Her eyes were of the same heavenly blue as the blue above but they were not gentle.

'There's something I have to do,' she said.

'You're being very serious about it. It must be something important. Do you want to tell me about it?'

'I don't think so.' She looked steadily across at him: at the dark hair falling over his forehead; his sun-tanned face; his kind eyes. In school no one had ever minded Mr Moxby. He had never hit anybody or been angry. He had loved Alice and thought her beautiful and had never even spoken to her. That set him apart as the halo distinguishes the blessed saint. 'You might try to stop me.'

'Only if I thought it might harm you in any way.'

She shook her head.

'It wouldn't harm me. Only him.'

'I wonder – is it something to do with Alice?'

He talked about her as no one else did. At home her name was never mentioned. It was as if no one remembered her. But Mr Moxby did. He had come to her this afternoon because he wanted to talk about Alice. She admitted him to the emptiness of her lonely heart.

'It's to do with the man who. . . .'

'I thought it might be. You intend to punish him in some way?'

'To ruin him the way he ruined Alice and then kill him.' The intention was so deep-seated and familiar that she gave no particular emphasis to the dreadful words.

He almost smiled. It was so natural and childlike. A purpose impossible to fulfil could do her little harm. In time she would surely grow out of it. The number of times he had wanted to torture and kill Councillor Garson!

'Well, I understand the feeling.' His tone must have been that of an indulgent parent, he thought afterwards. 'You may find him some day if you go on looking.'

'There's no need to look,' she said. 'I know him.'

She was not smiling now; nor was he.

'How can you be sure?'

'Alice told me. She told me everything.'

# Chapter 23

Tilly went into the kitchen and closed the door. She felt safer there. She never used to be nervous but she had never been so much alone as she was now, without Mrs Ushart and then without the children. The other two were out most of the time. She hadn't seen a soul all day except the boy who brought a letter for the master from Councillor Garson. It was never daylight in the schoolhouse – nearly dark everywhere inside and you might as well be in prison for all you could see going on outside.

You got used to the geyser going wrong and having to boil kettles all the time and never getting to the bottom of the work. But people could work their fingers to the bone and it didn't make them nervous, just tired to death. There was this feeling she had now, all the time expecting something to happen. These long summer evenings were the worst. In winter as soon as it got dark and she had cleared up, she went to bed. In the inner wall of the kitchen a latched door opened on a staircase leading to her room. Once she was safely in the kitchen she could go up without seeing the other two again. The minute she got into bed she fell asleep. Whatever went on in the house after that she knew nothing about.

She crept nearer to the fire: with its thick walls the house was cool in summer. The fire was nearly out, but she was drawn to the hearth as her primitive ancestors had been drawn to theirs for protection against the terrors of the night. On this particular night it was not just nervousness that kept her crouching on the fender, her eyes on the door to the hall, her ears strained. She was frightened.

The other two were together in the living room. Tilly had gone to see if the master had finished his supper and was clearing away the things, not that he'd eaten much, when they heard Etta close the front door. She did not go straight upstairs as she usually did. Tilly saw the master's face change as she came into the room. Never in her life had she seen such a look on a person's face until she turned and saw the same look on Etta's. It terrified her. She seized the tray and fled.

She had never given much thought to the relationship between the two whom she rarely saw together. She had remembered the master's warning that Etta was not to be believed if she said things that couldn't possibly be true but Etta hardly said anything. She did her share of the housework which was much smaller than Tilly's but most of her time was spent elsewhere. They had been three separate people, or so it had seemed.

But seeing them like that, she knew that the other two were connected in some terrible way that she didn't understand. That look united them. She could not have described it but she knew what it meant.

It was a look of murderous hatred.

The two confronted each other as they had done once before. He had known then that she was as unyielding as a rock: a latter-day Medusa who could turn human beings to stone with one petrifying stare. He had been confident in those days and could toy lightly with classical allusions. She had given no sign then that she knew of his unfortunate entanglement with her sister. To think of it in such terms was to evade the truth: he was acutely aware that it had been much worse – very much worse. Nevertheless when it was over his mind had been at ease, his reputation unblemished – until Etta came back and made him take her in.

Since then there had not been a day, an hour, a minute when he had not been reminded of Alice Hood. She too had come back: no phantom but in the living breathing flesh he had held in his frenzies of frustrated passion, until she became a threat to his career, his prestige, and to his marriage. Her death should have saved him. It had merely allowed him time to forget her, so that her resurrection had found him disarmed and unprepared for a conflict he could not win.

'Every time you see me,' Etta had said, 'you'll think of Alice.' He also thought of her constantly when he was alone. The two girls, one dead, one venomously alive, had become fused to form a constant threat. It was driving him mad as Etta had intended.

'Remember, I have only to tell what Alice told me. . . .'

He wondered if she had in fact told Madeline, whose contempt for him could scarcely have been increased by the revelation, or by any other.

The torture was clearly meant to last. It was to be life-long. To bring it to an end one of them must die. This was a critical moment. The note in his pocket was from Garson telling him that Birkett was dead. It signalled his escape from the suffocating pressures of a place he had himself defiled. All that prevented him from seizing the opportunity was the girl in front of him, so near that he could reach out and strangle her: golden-haired, white-skinned, red-lipped, capable of destroying him as Alice had been; like Alice in every way but one. Alice was already dead: this one not yet.

'I've seen Mr Moxby,' she said. 'He told me that you want to marry Miss Kent. You won't be marrying her. You must tell her. It will be uncomfortable for you but you'll have to do it quickly before it is formally announced.' That was Mr Moxby's phrase. 'I don't want her to be humiliated. Tell her tomorrow or I shall have to tell her why you aren't fit to marry anyone.'

For her too it was a critical moment. She had known that there would come a time when she would have to do more than torture him. There would be a sign, warning her that the time had come. She felt that it was near. Mr Moxby was clever enough to work out for himself who it was that had wronged Alice and caused her death: she had not told him. If others should find out, her secret would be of no more use: Ushart would be ruined anyway. But it was important to save Miss Kent from making a mistake that would ruin her too. She fingered the keepsake at the neck of her blouse as she had often done when she was lonely and afraid.

He had not spoken. Absorbed in her own calculations, Etta had no inkling of the fury he was rigorously holding in check: it was like swallowing bile. Her thinking was callous but uncomplicated: she had grown used to having him at her mercy. She had not foreseen that between two people who hated each other the intention to kill could be mutual too.

# Chapter 24

At The Birches next morning preparations for Mrs Liffey's visit were complete. The bed in the spare room was graced with the best honeycomb quilt, every stitch put in by hand, and valances with crocheted edges eight inches deep. Fresh lavender bags scented the drawers. In the larder there were boiled ham, a pressed tongue, a homemade beef-and-ham brawn, junkets and custard tarts. The weather was too warm for jellies.

'You'd think she was expecting a tribe of hungry warriors,' Aggie muttered to Gladys. 'Let us hope all that meat will keep. There's thunder in the air. The milk'll turn for sure.'

Cedric and his mother arrived in time for an early lunch. He would leave with Aggie in the evening and return on the following Saturday to take his mother home. It was chiefly due to Cedric that everything went off pleasantly. His mother was not used to long drives and felt a trifle queasy. Mabel, like Aggie only more acutely, feared the effect of thunder on her pressed tongue not to mention the leg of lamb for Sunday. Lorna was uneasy on account of a decision she had made and meant to act upon before the day was over.

Cedric alone was genial and at ease. For him life on the whole was good. He had survived the post-war years more successfully than many others of his cruelly depleted generation and had devoted himself to restoring the family business. His patient

kindness made him a valuable member of the small and ener-
getic group including Faith Wilbur who saw the end of the war as
the beginning of a new era in Donnerton. Their efforts to
improve on the old one were slow to produce results but their
enterprise did enliven the city.

After lunch he strolled round the garden: he found three
sagging stakes in the back fence and hammered them into place;
took possession of the garden shears, declared them sadly in
need of sharpening and promised to bring them back next week
in mint condition together with a new washer for the kitchen tap;
advised Aunt Mabel to sell her shares in textiles and put the
money into government bonds, and got out the deckchairs.

'It's a real treat to have a man about the place again.' Aunt
Mabel lay back in the shade to sigh over the long years of her
widowhood. She would lose Lorna too: it was bound to happen,
although Lorna seemed slow to realize that a young man might
have other things to do on a Saturday besides driving his mother
from Donnerton to Canterlow when she could easily have come
by train.

Lorna did realize that Cedric was too good a friend to be kept
in the dark about her engagement. She and Adam had agreed
not to announce it until September when a whole year would
have passed since Madeline's death but Cedric of all people must
be told. She did not admit to herself why this must be so or why
it was going to be difficult. So far there had been no opportunity
to talk to him alone as both the older ladies were aware.

'Why don't you two go for a walk?' Mrs Liffey suggested from
her deckchair. 'Then Mabel and I can doze off if we feel like it.'

'I've often thought of that walk we took along Fold Lane,'
Aunt Mabel said with some exaggeration. 'Belle was not well. Do
you remember, Lorna? What with one thing and another I never
heard whether there was a good crop of Grenadiers on that tree
in the Hammonds' garden.'

'It's too early for apples,' Cedric said.

216

'Too soon for gathering although the Grenadier is early ripening. Such a waste to let them fall. If you happened to be here when they're ready, you could drive us there and back. It's too far to carry a load of apples.' She was growing sleepy. Dora had already closed her eyes.

'Your aunt seems keen on apples,' Cedric remarked.

'They want to get rid of us.' Half-amused, Lorna nevertheless felt the choice of walk ill-omened. The associations of that particular Sunday evening would always be disturbing. 'But it's quite a long way and they'll be disappointed if we're not back for tea.'

Cedric's sensible suggestion that they should drive part of the way also had its drawbacks. To sit close to him while she confided the news of her engagement to someone else seemed unsuitable somehow: remarks could be dropped more casually as they sauntered in the open air, but sauntering would certainly make them late for the handsome tea Aunt Mabel had provided.

In effect they were no sooner in the car than they were out of it, at the point where the grass path led from Fold Lane to the Hammonds' house. All the same there had been a perfect opportunity for raising the subject uppermost in her mind. Its urgency was increasing at the same rate as her reluctance to introduce it.

From sheer weakness of will she had hurriedly pointed out one or two houses of no distinction whatsoever as being 'rather interesting' before launching into an account of the Hammonds and her meeting with Julian, the one survivor of the brotherhood.

'Will he be there, do you think?' Cedric was interested.

She knew only that he had intended to return in the summer. Once or twice she had set out on a walk in this direction but for one reason or another had turned back. There had been so much to occupy her that she had almost forgotten Julian Hammond. Here in the seclusion under the trees was an opportunity to tell Cedric, what had been occupying her mind for the past months. She must do it now, at once.

'That must be the house.' Cedric had caught sight of a chimney with smoke rising. 'The fellow must be there.'

If so, this was not the time to begin on the delicate matter of her engagement. In two minutes they had reached the gate.

As always one's impression was of the silence, a factor more positive than the mere absence of noise. It lay oppressively on the air, forcing one to listen for some sound however slight until anticipation became foreboding. Vines shrouded walls and eaves as if they had strangled life out of a house from which all human life had already gone. Through their clinging leaves lightless windows peered at the overgrown garden. Cedric knocked. There was no response. Lorna tried the door. It was unlocked but she closed it again with scarcely a sound.

'It's over there. The tree, by the wall.'

They went through long grass, releasing clouds of gossamer-borne seeds and treading on the bird-pecked windfalls. There would be a poor crop of Grenadiers this year. Lorna remembered how confidently she had bitten into one and how bitter had been the taste. She knew better now than to expect sweetness: it was not to be counted on but to be valued all the more dearly when found.

'It's been neglected.' Cedric was speaking of the tree. 'If there's overcropping when a tree is young, it hasn't the strength left for putting out new wood. In another year or two the apples will be no bigger than crabs. It's sad,' he went on rather unexpectedly, 'a place as neglected as this when you think of all the care and planning and laying out of the garden over the years. There's a terrible amount of waste in the world: a lot of striving that comes to nothing. I suppose that's why they had to invent heaven.' He had seen the greatest waste of all at close quarters and had drawn his own conclusions about heaven.

'Cedric! It was you. Do you remember? You wrote it in my autograph book. "A man's reach should exceed his grasp. . . ." '

' "Or what's a heaven for?" I remember what a struggle I had to find something suitable. I must still have had hope in those distant days. . . .' Looking down he saw her eyes fill with tears. 'What is it, Lorna? There's something wrong, isn't there? Why don't you tell me? You know I'd do anything to help' – he steadied his voice – 'even keep away if that was what you wanted.'

'Oh Cedric, I've been trying all day to tell you. . . .'

She was startled by the opening of the gate and turned to see Julian Hammond.

'Miss Kent!' He had come nearer, then hesitated. 'Am I disturbing you?'

'That's a very nice way of putting it.' With an effort she spoke lightly and made the introductions. 'This is Julian Hammond, Cedric, on whose property we are trespassing with a view to helping ourselves to his apples later on. I did ask you if it would be stealing – do you remember? – and you didn't answer.'

'You didn't need to ask.'

Once again he was carrying a sack of kindling. In country clothes and open-necked shirt he bore so little resemblance to the man in black whom she had seen in the station that she gave no thought, just then, to the suspicions she had not so much formed as dallied with. He seemed more cheerful than on the winter day when they had drunk milkless tea and talked in the firelight.

'That would be your car I saw in Fold Lane. A Wolseley 15hp. How do you find it?'

Naturally Cedric told him in some detail. Inevitably they forgot her.

'We're boring you,' Julian said. 'By the way, I should explain. This is the first time I've been here since I saw you.' He had been appointed land agent to an estate in Dorset. The house was to be sold at last to a firm of architects interested in restoration. The land alone made the property worth buying. 'This will be my last visit. I'm glad we met. You'll come in and have a cup of my famous tea?'

'Thank you, but Aunt Mabel will be expecting us.'

'Lorna's Aunt Mabel is also responsible for this intrusion on your privacy.'

'A man can have too much privacy. As a rule there isn't another human being to be seen here from dawn to dusk. Today has been an exception. Four people in one afternoon is a record.'

'Two others besides us?' Lorna remembered the other two who had made her first visit to the Hammond house so significant. The memory of it helped to increase the tension she had been feeling all day.

'A girl and a man. Not together. The girl is down there by the dam, sitting there and gazing at the water. She must be waiting for someone.'

'Had you seen her before?' More hung upon the answer than he could know.

'No. I don't know any of the local people.' And yet there had been something about the girl to stir a memory, as fleeting as the feeling in a strange place that one has been there before. 'I turned back when I saw her and didn't have a close look.'

'And the man?'

'He was coming from Canterlow. Perhaps he was the one she was waiting for.'

He must have forgotten the clockmaker's daughter, remembering only that he hated the very thought of her. He had probably done her no harm and did not deserve the harm she had unknowingly done him. She had been the cause of his quarrel with Digby whom he had loved as he would never love again. He had not been granted time to make amends. It had been a tiny episode in Armageddon, the supreme conflict of nations, but it had left a wound that would never heal.

He told them of a quicker way back to the car by a path skirting the outer garden wall. They shook hands and wished him well in his new appointment. At the corner Lorna looked back and waved. He raised his hand in a farewell salute. That was how she would always remember him – alone, with the house dark and empty behind him.

They found the short cut but in doing so passed, on the other side of the track, the path leading down to the dam.

'It must be Etta,' she explained. 'I can't think it right for her to be sitting there alone. It wouldn't take more than five minutes to go down and speak to her. We might lure her away with the offer of a ride in the car.' It was a forlorn hope. When was Etta ever lured?

'Shall I round up the man and offer him a lift too? We may as well make a clean sweep of the countryside while we're at it.'

'I'm not interested in the man. He can look after himself whoever he is.' It was a heedless remark as she was soon to realize.

They made their way at first through brushwood but the path widened as they came out into the open and saw below the gleam of water, no longer golden as she remembered it but leaden grey under a heavy sky. They had reached the gnarled hawthorns where she had seen Alice Hood and her lover when Cedric caught her arm.

'Just a minute. There's something going on down there. She's not alone.' They heard a voice, a cry quickly muffled. 'You wait here.'

He went quickly down, over the low wall and across the grass to the dam. Lorna caught a glimpse of white and followed with a sense of fatality, half-believing that the place itself was disaster-ridden.

In one respect at least Fate was merciful: she was just too late to see the worst of it. To have seen the dreadful act itself – and without warning – would have been too harsh a blow, a distortion too sudden, like the hideous mockery of a familiar face in a fairground mirror.

There had been a frantic struggle on the very edge of the dam.

It was over when she arrived. Roy Moxby had come running along the path from the direction of Fordham, in time to save Etta. The man lying in the water where Roy's furious blow had left him, ashen-faced and bleeding, was Adam.

Etta had got unsteadily to her feet, still dazed. She had a peculiar look with locks of her long hair wound tightly, rope-like round her throat. Her forearms were bruised, her blouse was torn. Lorna ran to comfort her as she had once failed to do years ago. Again she was too late. It was to Roy that Etta stumbled, to cling to him in the first flood of tears she had been seen to shed since Alice's death. He held her close and gently unwound the coils of hair from her neck.

'You certainly hit him.' Cedric spoke with zest. 'What on earth was he trying to do?'

A few words from Roy made the situation clear, though not the whole of it.

'She knew too much,' he concluded. 'I shouldn't have let it happen. I was nearly too late.'

Ushart had raised his head and shoulders out of the water and propped himself on one arm. For one stark moment as Lorna stared at him in disbelief, their eyes met. His had the hard glitter of green glass. They conveyed no message, held no appeal such as a man in extremity might make to the woman he professed to love, who had pledged herself to marry him, comfort and care for him.

Sick at heart, she faced the truth she had been eluding ever since the pledge was given. Whatever there had been between them, it could not have been love. How could it have been when in seconds he had become an object of revulsion? If she had really loved him, she would now be kneeling at his side. Instead she turned her back on him, deeply ashamed. Appalled as she must be by his cruelty and deceit, the shame was for her own miserable failure to see things as they really were. Nor could she escape – or ever forget – the sadness that comes when an illusion dies, leaving no more than the memory of a lost Eden. She felt all at once lonely.

As for him, though their eyes had met, he had not seen her: she might not have been there any more than the various other young people who had intruded on him. He was not entirely there himself. Indifferent to his bleeding face and to the chill of water, he was alone, racked by a private agony, tormented by a single image. No one else existed. She occupied his mind and heart more insistently than ever in life, confronting him in the depths of his shame. He had persuaded himself that she did not – could not – know what he had done that other time. Wakeful at her side as she slept, he had writhed in terror lest she should find out. No one knew. Yet he had been haunted by a suspicion that she did know: had not needed to be told. It was sufficient that she knew him and what he was capable of: knew him utterly, better than he knew himself.

Now it was no longer a suspicion. The long deception was over. Stripped of every device on which it had depended, he lay as if naked, exposed to an unflinching confrontation with the truth about himself and what he had done. Every manoeuvre to escape it had been futile, including the vestige of hope that she had not known. He was sure now that she had known. The external world was lost to him. She alone occupied the place he had ceased to see. For him the air itself, the vast space between leaden sky and fatal water was filled with Madeline's silent contempt.

'Is it someone you know?' Cedric had seen Lorna's distress.

Enlightenment had been so sudden, the reversal of feeling so complete that she had to force herself to believe that she was seeing again the man she had seen with Alice Hood. At that time she had seen no more than part of him – his arm, his hands – and had ever since detested him for his heartlessness while at the same time lavishing on the same man all her devotion. She had been as helplessly his victim as Alice had been, ministering to his self-esteem as Alice – who could know in what circumstances? –

had gratified his physical need. And now he was struggling to his feet, a spiritless creature, sullen and self-pitying.

'I thought I did,' she said, 'but I was wrong. I didn't know him at all.'

It served her right. She ought to have known. A more perceptive woman would have interpreted Madeline's sparse hints as warning signs and sensed his falseness. It was still too soon to grasp, as she did later, the full extent of his monstrous egotism. The thought of his relationship with Alice revolted her. Only a selfishness bordering on the abnormal could have sustained his double life, untouched by remorse. In time, all she had been too naïve to see became apparent and could never be forgotten; but here – now – with the man in front of her, she was sickened by the sordid details of his guilt. He had planned with cold calculation to kill Etta by letting it be known that she was not of sound mind and without his protection might be found drowned as her sister had been.

She went across to Etta, took her by the hand and drew her away; produced a handkerchief and a comb from her own hair, covered her gaping blouse with her own linen jacket and did what she could to make her feel more normal – and found that some such change had already taken place. Etta had emerged from the ordeal shaken and frightened, but less unapproachable. She seemed younger, less austere, more fragile.

'He came from behind,' she said, her teeth chattering. 'I thought it was Mr Moxby come to talk about Alice again.'

'Mr Moxby saved you, Etta, thank God.'

'Yes,' she breathed, and put her hand to the red weals on her throat. 'Yes.' She smiled rather shyly and glanced across at him.

'What's all this about?' Cedric was demanding. 'Who is this man and what was he doing?'

'He was doing what I think he did to her sister.' Roy lowered his voice. Neither Lorna nor Etta must hear. 'Unfortunately that can never be proved now.'

'This was certainly attempted murder, wasn't it? He should be handed over to the police – and quickly.'

'As a matter of fact he'd be safer with the police. I rather like the idea of leaving him to crawl away and go on crawling for the rest of his life. Look here.' He addressed Ushart. The man's humiliation was abject: yet he remained resentful as if oblivious to the depths to which he had committed himself and Roy spoke brusquely – yet less savagely than he might have done. Some faint vestige of the daily life they had shared restrained him, even though all respect had gone. 'Once they hear about this in Canterlow, your life won't be worth living. In fact it won't last long. You know what happened at Canter Edge and Ezra Kirk was a good and decent man.'

Ushart had recovered sufficiently to stand upright.

'What have you in mind?' Blood dripped from his mouth to his chin. He brushed it away and more blood came.

'I thought we'd give him a couple of hours to collect his things and clear out.'

Roy glanced at Cedric for confirmation.

'I take it he isn't likely to murder anyone else.'

'Not now. He only does it to protect his reputation and that's gone for good. It was bogus anyway.'

Lorna did not hear these scathing remarks. She and Etta were already climbing the hill. Etta had submitted to being led away like a child but she had not forgotten that it was Miss Kent who needed comforting.

'You wouldn't have been happy with him,' she said. The understatement was also child-like, 'I had to stop it. I said that I would tell you about him and Alice and that's why he tried' – she paused as if she had not till then fully realized the enormity of it – 'to kill me.'

As comfort it was well intentioned. For Lorna it had the sting of an asp. If anything could have added to her misery it was to know that her unseemly engagement had brought about this near catastrophe. The infatuation had harmed others as well as herself.

'Knowing what he was like I had to stop it.' Etta was looking at her anxiously. There was only one thing to be said and she said it humbly.

'Thank you, Etta.' She kissed her cheek. 'You've been a true friend.'

They waited on the ridge for Cedric. Roy and Ushart had already gone. With Etta at her side she felt the strangeness of her involvement with the sisters and with the man who had made all three of them suffer, though she had suffered least of the three. She had behaved like a creature bewitched – by the dreamlike beauty of this valley and by her own longing for love. Enchantment, she thought, was a kind of madness: a failure to distinguish between seeming and being.

And now the sultry afternoon seemed endless, the air stagnant. She felt physically weak as after a long illness. The incident by the water had been so spectacular a deviation from normality that when the storm, long brewing, broke at last, it seemed to give the final touch of melodrama.

The scene had changed, the sky grown lurid. Trees on the far side of the dam had darkened and hills, black-rimmed, moved closer. She flinched as the first fork of lightning flickered from sky to water. From heaven to earth? In the circumstances she could be forgiven for wondering if in the ruin of the man who had caused her death Alice Hood was being avenged. Perhaps for once she was right. The clap of thunder overhead seemed to confirm that Nature itself had been outraged.

Then like a blessing came the first cool drops of summer rain. They fell on leaves and flowerheads and on her upturned face. Amid the confusion of thought and emotion that troubled her she felt her wounded spirit respond to a new sensation and recognized it as a feeling of relief. The spell was broken. She was free to leave.

*

'You have had a long day, Mr Moxby.' Miss Craig had brought his bedtime drink, reheated for the third time.

She advanced to place the tray on the table, her movements a trifle slower than usual though they were never quick, and lingered to adjust the doily and rearrange the three Shrewsbury biscuits. He was aware of being given time to tell her why his day had been longer than usual. She was much too refined to ask.

'Thank you, Miss Craig.' He held the door open for her.

'Good night, Mr Moxby, and God bless you.'

'And you too, Miss Craig. Good night.'

Rumours, circulating wildly, had already reached Church Lane where it was known that Tilly had left the schoolhouse that morning and fled to her uncle at Goosegreen Farm; that Miss Kent, Etta Hood and a young gentleman had arrived at The Birches in a car and yet all three of them were soaked to the skin; that Mr Moxby had seen Mr Ushart off on the seven o'clock train with a small suitcase. Apprised of these facts, Miss Craig had prepared a nice little supper for Mr Moxby after his long day, alas to no avail. He was unable to eat a bite, having been ruthlessly regaled at The Birches with cold meats needing in view of the weather to be consumed at once.

Roy was tired but did not expect to sleep. Was it right to let Ushart go? He had felt instinctively that legal proceedings would have caused as much distress to others as to the man himself: to the children, to Lorna, above all to Etta, as news of the attack on her might have raised new questions about the death of her sister. His own suspicions had no foundation, nothing that could constitute evidence, except that he had seen Alice dead and had seen the marks of attempted strangulation on Etta's neck.

Lorna had seen the man in black walk away – or seem to. She had not seen where he went or whether he had stayed concealed. He could have been as desperate then as he was today. There could have been an earlier scene by the dam, similar to the one he himself had interrupted, but more successful.

The truth could never be known. It was suicide, they said in Canterlow. But for the rest of his life he would be troubled by the suspicion that Alice had not been alone when she died and that her death had not been by drowning.

# Chapter 25

'It was a mirage.' Faith spoke with authority though well aware that she had not heard the whole story. 'So far as I know, no one was ever ashamed of seeing one.'

'But they're usually in deserts. . . .'

'Yes. The lost traveller, longing for water, actually sees it – a whole shimmering lake – and then it's gone.' The time, the place and the longing were all there, she thought. In Lorna's case the longing was to love and be loved. 'An optical illusion,' she went on firmly, 'caused by the curving of rays of light in an atmosphere of varying density. We were made to learn definitions at school to correct vagueness in our thinking. There's a special kind of mirage called *fata Morgana* when objects appear magnified and blurred in their outlines. Does that sound familiar to you?'

'I do see what you're driving at.'

'I'm sure there must be a psychological equivalent. You saw what wasn't there, that's all.'

'I certainly did.'

'A girl can't help it if nature plays tricks on her; and surely it was to your credit that you created something better than the actual object, though as a rule I don't believe in trying to improve on nature.' She looked round. The new crèche reeked of fresh paint. As a challenge to the gloom outside walls and woodwork had been given several coats of yellow. The curtains were yellow too. 'Simulated sunshine. It does work, I admit.'

It was noon on a Saturday. The bags of washing had gone to the laundry. All the toys had been washed and put on racks to dry. The young assistant had gone home. All the infants had been collected except the one in Lorna's lap. After the morning's din it was restful to be lectured by Faith who had dropped in to see that all was going well.

'You're doing me good,' she said.

'But wait, there's more to come. This is the best part. The weary traveller trudges on until at last he comes to a real oasis with real palm trees and real pure water, a great deep well. It has been there all the time, waiting for him.'

'You've turned it into a parable, haven't you?'

'I won't deny it. Incidentally I thought we didn't approve of dummies.'

At the abrupt change of subject they both laughed.

'We don't, but Daisy is an exception.'

'She's exceptionally good.'

'Because of the dummy.'

'Or because of being nursed with so much love?'

'There's a special bond between Daisy and me. We neither of us ever knew our mothers. Her mother didn't live long enough to see her. There are five others at home. Two of them have ringworm. Cathie, the eldest, is twelve. She looks after them all – and her father. She'll be here presently.'

'Is Daisy to be the baptismal name?'

'I think so. Cathie told me, "We just knew the minute we saw her that she was Daisy".'

'It would be worth waiting to see Cathie but I must go. Is Cedric coming for you? I wish he could see you looking like Raphael's Madonna.' Not that he could worship me more than he already does, she thought with a pang of loneliness.

'In an apron with my hair coming down?' Lorna was vain

enough to hope that Cathie would come in time for her to make herself presentable – and as Faith left, the child arrived, having run all the way, a waif-like creature in a frock too thin for the day, her arms bare, her hands reddened with scrubbing and washing.

'I had to get dinner on.' She took her sister with the competence of an experienced mother. 'She's the best of them all for not crying. See you on Monday, miss.'

Lorna watched her go back to the other four, the dinner, the two cases of ringworm and to a future of ceaseless toil – and hastily emptied her pockets of safety pins, clean rags for nose-wiping, a jar of Vaseline, scissors, a few wrapped fruit-gums, and had tidied her hair by the time Cedric appeared. He checked that all the windows were fastened and the taps turned off while she collected her belongings.

'Yellow is a good colour but haven't you rather overdone it?' he said as they took a final look round.

'It's a well-known fact that small children like yellow.'

'Then they must be very happy here – and dazzled too – and so are you, I believe.'

'Dazzled?'

'Happy.'

'Yes.' She had regained her natural serenity and with it an added softness. As yet he did not know that her gentle thoughtfulness was more particularly for him than for the world in general as he modestly supposed. 'Much happier than I deserve to be. . . .'

On Donner moor the heather was rust-brown, the bracken bronze and gold. After lunch at the Stormcock Inn they had the whole vast sweep of it to themselves under a wide sky with slow-moving clouds, dove-coloured against the pale blue of early autumn. They took the path to the viewpoint, Burnhope Rock. It was wide enough most of the way for them to walk side by side.

'That day at Canterlow,' Cedric said suddenly. 'You were going to tell me something. What was it – or have you forgotten?'

Lorna hesitated. She had not forgotten and had been profoundly thankful that the disclosure had never been made. She had told no one of her engagement to Adam Ushart, not even Faith. How Etta had come to hear of it she had no idea and would have been enraged if she had known that Councillor Garson was responsible. When Aunt Mabel had at last heard the rumour, she made short work of it. Her niece would never have had anything to do with such a man as Adam Ushart had turned out to be. That particular rumour was scotched. There were plenty of others to take its place.

Lorna, whose probity could as a rule be relied on, was prepared in the matter of her engagement to cast honesty to the winds. There are some things a woman is entitled to keep to herself. Wild horses would not drag the truth out of her. Indeed the truth was becoming blurred in outline in true *fata Morgana,* fashion. She had almost succeeded in persuading herself that no such engagement existed. An understanding was all it had been: he had given her no ring; it was all quite unofficial. In any case the scale of his deception was such as to exonerate her from any obligation. Faith would have dealt with such a situation in a straightforward and upright fashion – though Faith would never have been embroiled in such a situation. She could never emulate Faith's integrity, only regard it with awe and admiration. Meanwhile her lips were sealed. It did not occur to her that her total silence regarding the man whom everyone else was talking about was more eloquent than words, but it had occurred to Cedric.

The day he referred to had been a turning point in her life and not only because Adam Ushart's true nature had been so startlingly revealed. Shame for her own folly was quickly followed by gratitude that the revelation had been made in time to save her from a crisis worse even than what she deserved, but learning the truth about Ushart was not the only discovery she made that day, nor the first, nor even eventually the most important.

The mirage, as Faith had aptly called it, had by that time already faded. She had stepped closer to reality from the moment he asked her to marry him and had never been at ease until the disastrous end. But the real cause of her unease had become apparent in the garden at the Hammond house.

'I still had hope in those distant days,' Cedric had said. . . . 'What is it, Lorna? Why don't you tell me? You know I'd do anything to help, even keep away if that was what you wanted.'

The quiet concern for her, the deep unselfishness, the rare unsteadiness in his voice had touched her to the heart. She knew then why it had been so hard to tell him of her misguided attachment to someone else. Cedric was closer to her than Adam Ushart had ever been or could ever be. They had grown up together; he had always been there – and she had paid no more attention to him than to the familiar features of the physical world, taking him for granted like the rising and setting of the sun and moon and the sequence of the seasons. As a girl she had been intrigued by the mystery of love and had failed to recognize its constant presence in her daily life.

Now he had asked a perfectly natural question and naturally expected an answer. The need to say something and at once had the effect of making her walk more quickly. The path had steepened and grown rougher. The walk had become a climb. Not far ahead Burnhope Rock squatted black against the pure sky. Already they were in its shadow. The moorland breeze was fresh, the air thin. It cleared the mind of inessentials. It was not the time nor was it the place to speak of false perceptions, devious scheming, cruelty, lies and betrayal, all of which must be evoked by the mere mention of Ushart's name. She must find something to say: neither tell everything nor say what would be untrue.

The stones underfoot were weatherworn and smooth. She chose the quicker, steeper way to the rock and walking carelessly, almost fell.

'Watch where you're going. That isn't the way.' He seized her hand and was electrified by the radiance of her smile as she came close to him. With her hand in his, she was a child again among strangers on a crowded beach, confused and frightened by the white breakers and the hungry surge of the sea, until he found her and took her back to safety.

'Cedric, dearest. You haven't changed.' She reached up and kissed him. 'It was just the same that day at Carlin Bay. Do you remember? I was lost and you found me. What would I do without you? Don't ever leave me.'

'You've been lost again, haven't you, love?' The wealth of tenderness in his voice brought tears to her eyes. 'How could I ever leave you? I've loved you all my life and even if you didn't want me, I'd go on loving you.'

They stood together on the flat top of the rock with the world at their feet and looked down to where in the distance the air thickened to form a grey pall. Beneath it lay the city, soot-grimed and shabby, teeming with warm and vigorous life.

'It's wonderful,' Lorna said, taking it to her heart again with all its imperfections. 'And after all that's where we belong.'

'Together,' he said, and no single word was ever fraught with so much meaning. It expressed the supreme satisfaction of homecoming after a difficult journey. It bore the weight of years in which he had waited without hope, dreading that she had found someone else; it conveyed the wonder of his transformation to 'dearest Cedric' and the joy that their first kiss had been hers, freely given – all culminating in the fixed determination never to let her go.

Looking down, he saw the haze above the city feebly sunlit. For him it shimmered as if reflecting the brightness of pure gold.

# Envoi

Fortunately the day, early in May, was warm and dry and Nora Webber was able to sit out of doors. After the exertion of the day before she was rather tired but it would have been too bad if she had had to stay in the house when every passer-by would have something to say about the wedding – or to ask, for Nora had been a guest. A car had been sent for her and her mother. They had sat with Miss Prior and Miss Ellwood in the pew immediately behind the relations of the bride and groom.

All had agreed that Lorna took after her father, a handsome gentleman who had come from America to give his daughter away. According to Gladys at The Birches, Mrs Hobcroft had been overheard to say that a person cannot very well give away what he cast aside nearly twenty years ago. Still, it was thought to be the prettiest wedding ever seen in Canterlow and now that it was over, life would be rather flat. It would be a year at least before Roy and Etta could afford to marry but Nora had already started on a few things for Etta's bottom drawer.

Mrs McNab, once housekeeper at the schoolhouse, had written to Mrs Hobcroft who let it be known that Mr Ushart was going to Australia where there were openings for experienced schoolmasters from the Old Country. It was good riddance, Councillor Garson said: he had always known that the man was a scoundrel and Miss Prior confessed that she had quite lost faith in him when he handed over the checking of the registers to Mr

235

Shackleton. The children were to stay in Scotland. Very little of interest could be said of the new master and his wife, a serious middle-aged couple thought to be on the mean side. She was said to knit every garment she wore, except her corsets presumably, and you could tell by one look at her that it was true.

These and other items of news were exchanged and exhausted over the Webbers' iron railings as the drowsy afternoon wore on. It was almost tea-time when Nora, having closed her eyes for a few minutes, opened them to see a man standing at the gate.

'Miss Webber?'

He was young, still in his twenties, she thought, but he appeared to be in poor health. His skin, which should have been pink in keeping with his fair eyebrows and blue eyes, was of a pale coffee colour and his hair was bleached and faded. He looked as if he had been left out in strong sunshine and forgotten. His manner was drooping and despondent.

'I was told that you might be able to help me. Do you know of anyone who would take me as a lodger?'

'Do you know Canterlow?' His features and voice were vaguely familiar.

He had known it before he went abroad, he said, to China, where he had worked in the mission field until his health broke down. He had preached more than once in Canterlow and liked the place.

On the garden seat with a cup of tea he revived and expanded a little. His life in China had been eventful, too much so, and sometimes violent. He had been advised to live quietly for a time, avoiding strain and excitement. He had thought at once of Canterlow, a place where decent, sober, god-fearing people could lead their blameless lives in peace, remote from the outside world: a place where nothing much ever happened.

'Yes, I see what you mean.' A hint of uncertainty had crept into Nora's voice. 'Now let me think. There's Mrs Winstock down by the mill. She has a room to let.'

'Would she take me, do you think? Peaceful surroundings are all I need. To tell you the truth, Miss Webber, I am weary of human error, wickedness and sin. I trust that in this quiet place my faith in mankind may be restored.'

'It's very quiet there, down by the mill.'

Quiet indeed, on the utmost edge of the town with nothing beyond but the valley of the Beam – Miller's Dam, the Hammond house, and at a little distance, Canter Edge.

'There shouldn't be anything there to disturb you.'

All the same something impelled her to touch the wooden arm of her chair as she spoke; and when, having thanked her earnestly, he trudged away, she felt a little uneasy on his behalf. He was so clearly a man who needed someone to take him in hand. . . .